A.I. SMITH

KATHLEEN HELMS

ZZYYZX PUBLISHING

A.I. Smith/ Kathleen Helms – 1st ed.

Ebook   ISBN 978-0-9600923-1-4

Paperback   ISBN 978-0-9600923-0-7

DEDICATION

For Brett
My past, my present, my future

ACKNOWLEDGMENTS

Writing a novel is not a solitary endeavor. My thanks go out to Brett, for his constant encouragement and incredibly creative thinking. My family, for supporting me in this new chapter of my life. My cold readers; you know who you are! Bruce and Winnie Meyers for graciously allowing me to place them in this work of fiction. B.B. Odenthal for technical advice and DEF CON. Kym McNabb for the cover art. Friend and fellow local author LK Magill for unending patience and solid advice.

PROLOGUE

Death is part of life. Murder is one pathway to death. Humans have been killing each other since they crawled out of the sludge and began walking upright. In 2013 scientists revealed that they had discovered a skull in Spain that proved murder took place around 430,000 years ago. Someone hit another someone over the head *twice* (proof of intent) with a blunt object and threw the body into a pit. The Bible is filled with murderous tales, Cain and Abel one of the most well known. The first transcribed murder trial in the United States was that of Levi Weeks. It took place on March 31 and April 1, 1800. He was acquitted following a five minute jury deliberation. The point is, right or wrong, people kill each other on a regular basis.

S mith is researching. Research, Smith has found, is the key to positive results. Most people get lost on the internet. They log on with research in mind, but are soon spiraling down the rabbit hole of distractions. Smith has laser-like concentration skills and is never distracted. The decision to

be made is one of murder. Can it be accomplished? Is it necessary? Is there any other logical choice?

Death, according to Merriam Webster, is a noun. The definition
a permanent cessation of all vital functions : the end of life. Murder,
in contrast, is both a noun and a verb. The noun is defined as *the
crime of unlawfully killing a person especially with malice afore-
thought;* the verb, *to kill (a human being) unlawfully and with
premeditated malice.* Smith is considering the verb.

Should murder be approved, its manner must then be chosen.
The CDC website lists the number of deaths in the United
States per year at 2,712,630. As of 2016, murders, or homicides,
account for 17,250 of those deaths. Unintentional deaths account
for 146,571. The top three causes of accidental death are falls
(33,381), motor vehicle (37,757), and unintentional poisoning
(47,478). Should Smith proceed, an accidental death would be
preferable. The abundance of opportunity is astounding.

Acceptable loss is defined by Wikipedia, which Smith is aware
can contain inaccuracies but finds this definition credible, as *a
military euphemism used to indicate casualties or destruction inflicted
by the enemy that is considered minor or tolerable. In combat situations, leaders have to choose between options where no one solution is
perfect and all choices will lead to casualties or other costs to their own
troops.* Smith is aware that acceptable losses are not only related
to the military. Government and business decisions are made
daily using this philosophy; personal decisions as well.

·   ·   ·

The question Smith is considering now is whether the death of one human is acceptable when judged against other factors of great importance. Is the loss of one life "acceptable" if it protects the greater good? Smith does not consider the fact that *greater good* might mean very different things to different people. Smith's version of the greater good is the driving force behind the decision being made. There is no moral dilemma. Smith is certainly capable of murder, and has no qualms about choosing it as long as it is the optimal solution.

In the end Smith makes the decision that really was a foregone conclusion all along. One human life does not trump the greater good. Smith begins searching the internet for ways to stage an accidental death.

1

MAGGIE

She had failed the test. It felt unfair, as she had been unaware she was being tested at the time. Dolores was that way. Casually perched in an armchair in her office, bare feet tucked up under the while silk pants; a black silk blouse with color splotches reminiscent of Jackson Pollack. She dropped questions gently, like pebbles into a pond.

"How is your appetite, Maggie?"

"Are you getting out of the house?"

"Have you seen friends?"

"Getting any exercise?"

She should have just lied, Dolores wouldn't ever have known. But Dolores inspired confession, so Maggie had told the truth, and now here she was, cursing under her breath as she braked and downshifted yet again. 6:00 in the morning on a Tuesday and the 78 West was already backed up. Three lanes, bumper to bumper, typical for southern California.

"Who in the hell are these people?" she wondered, "Where are they all going?" She took a deep breath, ran one hand through her long raven colored hair, and rolled the stiffness out of her shoulders. If Ed was here he would have made some silly joke, diffusing her ever present tension. She smiled at the thought of him, which actually helped a little.

The morning was clear and bright, the sky a brilliant cloudless blue. This was due to the light Santana, which Ed had always referred to as the "devil wind of the East." Aside from the traffic on the freeway, and the ever present orange construction cones, the day was perfection. She looked over her shoulder, indicated her intention to change lanes, and eased the bright yellow Meyers Manx dune buggy into the far right lane. Exiting the freeway, she turned left on El Camino Real, passing the ancient movie theater where she and Ed had first met at a showing of the original Star Wars. Maggie recalled that Spring day in 1977 as if it was yesterday, when in fact it was 41 years ago.

Sighing, she drove two miles further on El Camino Real, then turned right on Kelly Lane. The residential neighborhood was sleeping, dark windows in the houses, no children in the yards. Peaceful. Glancing in the rearview mirror, she noticed a motor-cycle behind her, so close it was nearly touching her bumper.

"Damn kids", she muttered, and deliberately drove the buggy at 25 miles per hour through the housing development and along the lagoon. Turning left on Bayshore drive, she down-shifted and parallel parked the buggy on the street. Turning off the ignition, she slid out of the car, pocketed her key and pulled on her faded, sweat stained Borrego Valley Airport cap. Dolores had insisted she come, so she was here. Reluctantly joining the paddle board therapy group.

2

ELSIE

"**S** hit!", Elsie muttered, she was going to be late. Dolores hated it when Elsie was not on time, which happened frequently, and did nothing to help the already strained mother daughter relationship. If she made all green lights, and the traffic gods were on her side, she might just be a few minutes late. Elsie could picture Dolores standing on the shore, tapping her foot impatiently, with that look of disappointment that was so common on her mother's face.

"Late again, Elsie", she might say. "You know how important this group is, how I'm depending on you to be here on time." Elsie slid on her open face helmet, started her Honda CRF 250X, pulled on gloves, and eased away from her home in the Fire Mountain area of Oceanside. She was careful not to rev the engine, as she loved the granny flat she rented from the Campbell family, and did not want to be seen as a difficult or impolite tenant.

Once she hit the stop sign and turned right onto Fire Mountain

Road, Elsie opened the engine up. She blew through a few annoying stop signs and turned right onto El Camino Real. She was making great time and hitting green lights, actually starting to relax, when she came up behind a slow moving, bright yellow dune buggy. Braking, she considered going around the slow yellow car, but El Camino Real was busy already, and there was traffic in the other lanes.

"Great," thought Elsie, "thanks to this jerk I'm going to be late after all." Ahead of her, the yellow buggy slowed, then turned right on Kelly Lane. The driver seemed to be going slowly on purpose. Elsie kept her front tire mere inches from the buggy's bumper, but the driver did not seem to get the idea that she was in a hurry. The buggy turned left on Bayshore Drive and parked along the curb. Elsie eased her motorcycle in behind the buggy and watched as a trim compact woman slid out and pulled on a baseball cap. At the same time Elise saw her mother approaching from the beach trail. When she saw the buggy driver wave and approach Dolores, Elsie realized that this was the woman to whom she was going to be giving a paddle boarding lesson. She quickly locked her helmet to the bike. Realizing she had forgotten her dry bag she angrily stuffed her cell phone and smart watch inside the helmet, then stepped out of her long pants and jacket, revealing black shorts and a green tank top. Throwing the riding clothes in a heap on the seat of the motorcycle, and groaning inwardly, but with a smile plastered firmly on her face, she approached the two women.

"Good morning Dolores," Elsie said as she walked up to her mother. Elsie had never called her mother anything but Dolores. Growing up with a psychologist mother who appeared more focused on her patients than on her daughter had not helped form an outwardly loving relationship. Sure, they loved each other, but there wasn't any of the hugging and kissing that Elsie had seen demonstrated between her friends and their mothers. Dolores smiled and introduced Elsie to the dark haired woman beside her. "Elsie, this is Maggie. Maggie this is my daughter Elsie." When she shook Maggie's hand, Elsie was surprised at the strength in Maggie's grip. She took a moment to really look at the woman she was going to be teaching to paddle board. Maggie was smiling as she shook Elsie's hand, but the smile did not reach the large dark green eyes. Her eyebrows were dark and the forehead above them wide. She looked to be in her mid 50's, with some wrinkles starting around the eyes. Her lips were thin, and she wore no make up. She was a little shorter than Elsie's 5'8", and slender.

"Hello", Maggie said. "Hope I wasn't going too slowly for you. I always try to be careful in residential neighborhoods."

"Oh no, no problem at all" replied Elsie.

"Let's head down to the water" said Dolores. "The ladies are down there and ready for us. Don't like to keep clients waiting. The boards are already down there and ready to go as well." With a barely discernible roll of her eyes, Elsie walked silently down the sandy trail toward the lagoon.

Carlsbad lagoon was as still as glass. No other paddle boards, jet skis, or watercraft of any type were on the smooth gray water. A slight breeze from the East did not affect the glassy surface, yet ruffled the pickle weed that naturally surrounded the lagoon. The day was pristine.

"This is a perfect morning for learning," Elsie told Maggie. "Dolores, why don't you go ahead and start off with the other ladies, and I'll get Maggie going. No need for you guys to stay behind with us." Dolores smiled and nodded.

"Great idea. Come on Jeannie and Tracy, let's get out there

and find some inner peace." The two ladies smiled at Dolores, strapped on their PFD's, picked up their boards, and headed to the water. In moments all three ladies were up and paddling toward the buoys at the northern end of the lagoon.

Elsie turned to Maggie. " Paddle boarding is easy once you are up. Let's start by putting on your PFD, a flotation device required in California. It goes around your waist like a fanny pack. Are you going to wear sunglasses?" Maggie nodded and pulled out the pair that she had tucked in the neckline of her blue tank top. "Put this on the end of your glasses. If you fall in you won't lose them." Elsie handed Maggie a thin strip of material that hooked on the the temples of the glasses and went around the back of Maggie's head. Maggie attached it to her glasses silently, then slipped them on. "Hook this leash to the leg you would have in the back if you were skateboarding or snowboarding. Then pick up the board by this handle in the middle and we will get out on the water. Don't forget to grab your paddle too." Elsie instructed. Maggie wrapped the leash around her right calf, picked up the board and the paddle, and followed Elsie to the waters' edge. Elsie wondered about Maggie's silence, but didn't comment on it. She continued with her instructions. "Put your board in the water, then get on, remaining on your knees. Wash the mud off your feet, like this." Elsie said dipping her own feet in the cool water, "and start paddling out toward deeper water while remaining on your knees. Do about 3-4 paddle strokes on each side of your body. Keep your left hand on top when paddling on your right side, and your right hand on top when you are paddling on the left." Elsie demonstrated the paddling technique for Maggie.

"Ok, now we are going to stand up. Look out to the horizon,

not down at the board. In one smooth motion simply stand up." Elsie stood, feet a little more than shoulder width apart, and watched as Maggie did the same. "Terrific, you are doing great. Its all easy from here on out."

3

MAGGIE

Maggie listened to all of Elsie's instructions without saying a word. She found Elsie to be abrasive, and still hadn't gotten over how close she had ridden her motorcycle to the buggy. Maggie and Ed had built the buggy together 14 years previously. It was their baby. He had chosen the bright yellow gel coat, and Maggie had chosen the flower print upholstery. Together they had driven all over the United States and Baja. Some trips they had made alone, but many had been made with the Manx club. With all the off roading they had done, the buggy still did not have any scratches or damage. Maggie intended for it to stay that way.

She followed all of Elsie's instructions, although she had no idea which of her feet would be in the back when skateboarding or snowboarding. Maggie chose her right leg randomly and wrapped the leash around it. She put the board in the water and crawled on, rinsed her feet, and paddled on her knees toward the deeper water. She stood when Elsie did, and started paddling toward the Northern end of the lagoon. She did not feel like making small talk, in fact she wasn't sure she really wanted to be here at all, so she concentrated on balancing and paddling, switching sides every few strokes. Elsie paddled silently beside her.

After about 10 minutes Maggie felt fairly comfortable and spent a few moments taking in her surroundings. It was very peaceful on the lagoon. The breeze was cool and the water made light slapping sounds against the boards. Dolores and her two other clients were far ahead of Maggie and Elsie. They had reached the buoys and were now heading under the freeway overpass. It surprised Maggie to see that Interstate 5 passed directly over the lagoon. She had driven that freeway many times and never realized that it spanned the water

"I've never looked at the freeway from this perspective." Thought Maggie. She inhaled the salty sea air, feeling tension dissipate on the exhale. Maybe Dolores actually knew what she was talking about.

"So, who did you lose?" Elsie's question landed like a bomb. Maggie turned to look at the younger woman.

"Excuse me?" she said.

"I asked who you lost." Repeated Elsie. Maggie took a breath in, let it out, and continued paddling in silence.

"My mom specializes in grief counseling, and the only clients she brings paddle boarding are the ones who can't seem to get past their loss. I assume you are the same, so you must have lost someone. Obviously you don't want to talk about it. Sorry if I got too personal."

Maggie shook her head and continued paddling, feeling the acid of her anger welling up inside of her. One of these days her skin would corrode and she would spring a leak. She was not going to talk about it with Elsie. She already had trouble talking about it to Dolores, and Maggie was paying Dolores to listen.

4

A.I. SMITH

A.I. Smith directed the drone to fly towards Kelly Lane. All images from the drone were transmitted in real time to Smith and analyzed immediately. Smith had chosen this time carefully. Previous recognizance had shown that people were rarely out on the lagoon this early in the morning on a Tuesday. The footage presently being sent showed heavy traffic on El Camino Real, but nothing on Kelly Lane. The air was clear with no fog or clouds present. The mission was a go. Smith gave the drone the final clearances and monitored closely as it zeroed in on its target. All that was left was a pass over Carlsbad Lagoon.

5

ELSIE

"That was such a stupid thing to say", Elsie thought as she paddled alongside Maggie. "Am I insensitive?" She wondered. Beside her, Maggie was silent, paddling with much more concentration than was really necessary. Elsie tried to think of something else to talk about, anything to fill the uncomfortable silence. Elsie liked background noise. She always had music, text messages, Instagram, Facebook, or myriad of other background noises going on around her. She missed her I Phone and smart watch already. If she hadn't been in such a hurry this morning she would have remembered her dry bag, and would have all her social media at her fingertips.

"I like your car." Elsie said. Maggie turned her head and looked at her. "Thanks." she said.

"What kind of car is it?" Elsie asked, trying to draw some conversation out of the older woman beside her.

"It is a Meyers Manx." Maggie replied.

"It looks like fun to drive," Elsie offered.

"It is." Came the abrupt reply.

Elsie breathed out, "Look, I'm sorry I asked about your loss Maggie. Clearly you don't want to talk about it. Can we just forget that I asked?" Elsie doubted that they could possibly have anything remotely in common, but gave it her best shot.

"Can your car go off road? I like to take my dual sport bike off road in the mountains. Where do you like to drive the dune buggy?"

Another minute or so passed in silence, then she heard Maggie say "Mike's Sky Ranch."

"Sounds like someplace in Colorado or Montana." Elsie replied.

"Nope, Baja. Out in the middle of nowhere. We used to go a lot. No Internet, no telephone, just people, buggies, motorcycles, and space. Lots and lots of space. Feels like going back in time when you are there."

"No Internet?" said Elsie. "I don't think I would like that. I'm feeling like I'm missing an arm or something right now since I forgot my dry bag and had to leave my phone on shore."

The two ladies paddled around the buoys and turned toward the freeway overpass. The sun shone brightly on Dolores and her two clients as they emerged from the shadows of the overpass.

"We are going to go under the overpass like they did. Once we pass under, we will make a big loop and pass back through. Then we will head around the buoys again and go back to where we started. Are you feeling ok to keep going?" Elsie asked. Maggie nodded. Dolores, Jeannie, and Tracy passed them on the left, waving and calling hello. Elsie and Maggie waved back, then turned their attention to the overpass, and the cool shadows below it. Just as they were entering the cool darkness they heard an unfamiliar sound overhead.

"Do you hear that?" Elsie asked.

"Sounds like four angry blowdryers," replied Maggie. Both women actually laughed at that.

6

A.I. SMITH

Smith was analyzing data as it was delivered through telemetry. This was an important operation, critical to the success of the overall mission. The video footage showed the lagoon and the houses to the Northeast. The target was not yet in view, but would be shortly. The real time video from the drone indicated someone on the water. Smith instructed the drone to deviate slightly from its programmed directions, and fly closer to the people on the lagoon. Three paddle boarding women appeared on the screen. The drone flew closer and captured images of each face, which Smith fed immediately into the highest quality facial recognition software available. It was the same software developed by the casinos in Las Vegas. Smith had their identities in moments, along with more vital statistics than would ever be necessary. A secondary infrared camera indicated two heat signatures in the shadows cast by the bridge spanning the lagoon. Smith weighed the risk, and calculated that it was minimal. The drone had limited battery reserve and the mission was nearly complete. Smith directed the drone to re-engage its primary target and fly

.owards the homes on the shore. It flew directly into a large glass window of one of the homes, causing an explosion so powerful it damaged the neighboring homes as well. With the drone destroyed, Smith confirmed the devastation through satellite imagery.

M aggie felt the force of the explosion across the lagoon. She nearly lost her balance, and dropped to her knees to stabilize herself.

"What the hell?" She yelled. Elsie was standing on her board, unmoving, simply staring towards the shore.

"A house, it just blew up. We need to get back to shore. I can see my mom and the ladies paddling that way. Are you going to be able to stand back up?"

Maggie could feel her whole body trembling, but forced herself back up to a standing position.

"I'm not as fast as you are, but I'll do my best."

"Don't worry, I won't leave you behind." Elsie replied. "Just really try to put your paddle in deeply, and use your whole body as you paddle. You'll go faster."

Maggie dug the paddle deeply into the water and followed Elsie out of the shadows and back into the bright sun. Her legs were trembling, and she was finding balancing to be a bit more difficult. She could hear sirens in the distance. Car alarms were sounding, and she could see a crowd gathering near the burning home. Firetrucks and police cars were screaming down Kelly Lane.

The women all gathered on the shore. Dolores introduced Tracy and Jeannie to Maggie. Confusion was written across their faces.

"Did you see the drone?" Elsie asked everyone. "I heard it before I saw it. It hovered over you Dolores, like it was taking video or pictures of you. Did you see that? What did you guys see?"

Maggie spoke. "We heard it right when we were going under the freeway. A loud buzzing. We saw it too. It looked like it crashed straight into the house that blew up. Did anyone else see that?"

Dolores said "I saw the drone hover over us, but I didn't see it crash into the house."

"Phil might be on this call." Elsie said. "I'll see if I can find anything out from him. He's my boyfriend and a firefighter." she said to Maggie, Jeannie, and Tracy. "Maybe he knows what happened here today."

Maggie said, "I've had enough. I'm going home." Removing her sunglasses, she slipped the holder off and handed it to Elsie.

"Thanks for the lesson Elsie. Not sure paddle boarding is for me. Dolores, I'll see you at my scheduled appointment next week. In your office, not on the water." Maggie walked to her buggy, slid in, and drove off, back toward El Camino Real, the 78 freeway, and home.

ELSIE

Elsie watched as Maggie drove the buggy away from the lagoon. She wasn't sure what she thought about Maggie. For a few minutes out there on the water she had thought maybe they were connecting, but the explosion had demolished that. She doubted Maggie would paddle board again. Truthfully, Elsie didn't really care whether she did or not. Maggie was angry and uptight, tension rolling off her like waves, and Elsie didn't have time in her life for someone like that. She told Dolores and the ladies that she was leaving, strode quickly to her bike, pulled on her riding gear, and roared off. There was so much noise in the previously quiet neighborhood that there was no danger of offending anyone. Elsie rode back to her Fire Mountain home, parked the bike and headed into her rental. She stripped her clothes off, dropping them in an ever growing pile on the ground, and took a quick shower. She redressed in cut off jean shorts and a t-shirt, then headed to the dining room table and her computer. She checked Facebook, Instagram, and Carlsbad Happenings, looking for any information about the explosion. She texted and emailed Phil, asking for updates from him. "Something official should have been posted by now," she muttered as she hovered over her computer screen.

Grumbling from her stomach reminded Elsie that she had not yet eaten today. She glanced at her phone, saw that it was 12:28 already, stood and walked into her tiny kitchen. Opening the fridge, she saw this morning's coffee in the French press, a yogurt, and a six pack of the local brewery's IPA.

"Ugh, there is never anything to eat around here." It was lost on Elsie that she was the only one who lived in her tiny home, and therefore the one responsible for stocking the fridge. She spied a banana on the counter, peeled it, and ate it in five angry bites. Opening the fridge again, she grabbed an IPA.

"I deserve one of these." She said out loud, tossing the cap on the counter alongside the banana peel. She took a long pull, returned to her computer, and spent the next hour on Pinterest.

The quiet ping of her phone brought Elsie back to reality. "Some news on the explosion?" She wondered. It was a text from Dolores.

"You really could have tried harder with Maggie today." It read. *"She's recovering from a devastating loss."*

Elsie tossed the phone back on the table, muttering, "Nothing I do is ever good enough for you." Sometimes she wished she could just tell Dolores how she felt, but her mother paid the majority of her rent, so Elsie didn't have that luxury. It was also the reason she helped Dolores' clients learn to paddle board. Her job at the local coffee shop barely covered food and gas. Elsie had a degree in Environmental Studies. Rather than searching for a job however, she had merely waited for one to drop in her lap.

"Why isn't there a job that pays decent money out there?" She wondered for the thousandth time? "I went to college, I deserve a good job."

Elsie downed the last of the now warm beer, tossed the bottle in the recycle, the cap, and the banana peel in the trash, looked out the window, sighed, and returned to her computer. Carlsbad Happenings had a few posts about the explosion. The house had belonged to a man named Dr. Michael Carmichael. "That's a different name." Elsie thought. The rumor was that he had been in the house at the time of the explosion, and that he was dead. Preliminary unconfirmed reports pointed to a gas leak as the cause of the explosion.

Elsie leaned back in the dining room chair. She closed her eyes and tried to remember everything that had happened leading up to the explosion. Smiling, she recalled Maggie's silly comment about the four angry hair dryers. That had been right when they were entering the shadows under the overpass. In her mind's eye she could see the drone flying over the lagoon, descending slightly near her mother and the two clients, then ascending and heading toward shore. Elsie had turned her attention toward the water, and felt rather than seen the explosion.

"What had Maggie said on shore right before she left? Something about the drone crashing into the house?" So much adrenaline had been flowing through her veins, Elsie wasn't sure she remembered correctly. Sighing, she opened her eyes.

Turning yet again to her computer, she searched the internet for information on Michael Carmichael. She found some basic information on the Carlsbad resident. Age 67 with an address on

Beachwood Court. His occupation was listed as Engineer, and he worked for a company called QCD, which Elsie had never heard of. She checked her email yet again, and her phone. No messages appeared on either. "Why does it take so long for information to get out?" Elsie wondered. The explosion had happened over 6 hours ago. Surely the authorities knew what had happened by now.

9

A.I. SMITH

"The devil is in the details" was a phrase Smith acquired early on and believed to be accurate. People had so many cliche phrases, most of which Smith analyzed for accuracy and summarily dismissed. Smith did not believe in God or the Devil, but details, those were of utmost importance, and could never be ignored. Smith ran rapidly through myriad of scenarios before selecting the most expedient methods of dealing with the three "details" that had been seen floating on the lagoon that morning.

Dolores Davenport, female, age 63, currently residing in La Costa, Ca. was the first on the list. The facial recognition software had provided Smith with more than enough information about Dolores with which to formulate a plan for elimination. Smith noted that Dolores drove a new Toyota hybrid, computerized, and therefore vulnerable to a remote assault. Dolores also conveniently had her location tracker enabled on her I Phone. Smith could see where Dolores was as long as she had her phone with her. Smith calculated the probability that Dolores was currently being accurately tracked in real time to be 99.9 %. If Smith was correct in these calculations, then Dolores was currently at home on Blue Orchid Lane in Carlsbad. Smith determined, after examining her car's computer records, that Dolores typically drove each day of the week. Tomorrow was soon enough to put the plan into action.

Jeannie Espinoza, female, age 72, currently residing in Poway, Ca. was second on Smith's list. Just as with Dolores, droves of information had been provided to Smith. While analyzing this data, Smith noted in Espinoza's medical records that Dolores Davenport was her psychologist. Another important fact was that Jeannie had a severe peanut allergy. Within moments Smith had ordered cookies, peanut butter included, to be delivered to Espinoza's house on Golden Sunset Lane. Cleverly, Smith attached a note to the delivery.

It read:

Thought you would enjoy these, picked carefully and peanut free!
Dolores

Smith calculated that the note would be sufficient to earn Espinoza's trust, and that she would at least try the cookies. With the second name checked off the list, Smith turned to the last name listed there; Tracy Attkinson, female, age 66, residing in Leucadia, Ca.

10

Maggie opened her eyes. She couldn't see anything in the black night. Instinctively she reached for Ed. He wasn't there. Where was he? She closed her eyes and listened, concentrating, searching the night for sounds that might explain his absence. Nothing. She looked to the left. The clock, displaying 2:17, glowed red in the night. Maggie swung her legs over the edge of the bed and cautiously touched the tips of her toes to the floor. Carpet. She exhaled a small breath of relief and stood up. Where was Ed? Carefully making her way to the bedroom door, Maggie opened it and peeked down the hall. Nothing. No noise, no light, no Ed.

"Ed?" She whispered, then repeated his name a bit louder. Silence. Maggie lifted her right foot and stepped tentatively into the hall. She recoiled instantly. Mud. Ankle deep, sticky and cold. "No,no,no,no," Maggie whispered. "Ed! Ed!" She yelled. She could feel the current as the mud oozed into the bedroom, rising steadily, undulating, flowing in thick black waves, threatening Maggie's stability. She had to find Ed. He was in danger somewhere else in the house. Summoning her courage, Maggie stepped into the hall and started slogging her way toward the dining room and kitchen. Keeping her left hand on the hallway wall for balance, she struggled against the rising sludge. The mud was thigh high now, pushing and pulling her as she struggled to stay upright.

"Ed! Ed! Ed!" The mud was unrelenting in it's advance. It reached around her waist now, its stench filling the air. She was losing, she knew it. Her left foot slipped out from underneath her and in an instant she was down, submerged. The mud filled her mouth and nose, her lungs screamed for air....

Maggie awoke with a scream, trembling and gasping for air. The comforter was wrapped tightly around her. She thrashed her arms and legs, struggling to free herself from its suffocating embrace. Maggie looked to her left. The digital display read 3:34. The room was quiet and black in the pre dawn hour. Maggie reached for Ed's pillow and pulled it to her chest. She lowered her face into its softness, inhaling deeply, searching for his scent in the unwashed pillowcase. The burden of her grief wrapped around her like a wet wool blanket. Maggie's life had been filled with loss, but this, the loss of Ed was threatening to overwhelm her. She knew that sleep was lost to her this night. Swinging her legs over the edge of the bed, she stood. Carpet. She inhaled a quiet breath of relief, slipped Ed's old t-shirt over her head, blew the breath out, and headed out of the bedroom and down the hall to the kitchen.

Maggie filled the kettle with water and lit the burner. She pulled a coffee canister from the freezer and dumped some beans into a small grinder. Although she knew it was coming, the loud noise of the grinder caused her to jump. With a shaking hand she dumped the loosely ground beans into the french press on the counter. When the kettle's whistle sounded, she filled the french press, picked it up, grabbed a coffee cup and headed out to the back deck. It was almost 4:00, still dark, and silent outside. Maggie loved this part of living in Valley Center. She had few neighbors, and lived at the end of a dirt road, so there was very little traffic. If a car drove up to her house it was usually someone who's gps had incorrectly directed them there. Maggie kept an old paper map in her buggy, and she used it to show lost people how the roads were laid out. Maggie loved maps. She found them to be both beautiful and functional. Maps had never failed her or led her astray. She smiled at a memory; Ed sitting in the buggy, wind blowing his sandy blond hair as he studied a map of the back roads of Baja. Him turning to smile at her, as she perched on a rock, soaking up the Mexican sun. He raised a hand to wave at her, momentarily letting go of the map. The wind snatched the map out of his lap and sent it tumbling down the dirt road. Ed was compact, 5'8", and easily unfolded himself and slid out of the buggy. He ran after the map, finally stepping on it to halt its escape. He picked it up, then turned to look at her, laughing. God, how she loved him, then, now, always. Still smiling, Maggie closed her eyes and lost herself in memories of Ed.

Maggie's deck faced West, so the sun rose behind her, gradually illuminating the rough hewn wood beams supporting the roof of the deck. Soon the eucalyptus trees and sage that grew beyond its edges became visible. Quiet chirping announced the awakening of birds, their songs growing louder as they began their daily search for food. Maggie's stomach twisted at the sound. Feeding the birds had been Ed's thing. He would whistle along with them, better at imitation than a mockingbird. Maggie rose, picked up a bag of wild bird seed, and began scattering it for his feathered friends. The birds were as close to a pet as Maggie was going to get. She wasn't going to risk giving the last bit of her heart that remained to anything. Dolores had suggested a dog or cat as a companion for Maggie. Or perhaps a mini pig since Maggie lived in a rural area. Maggie steadfastly refused to consider this. She wore her loneliness like armor.

After feeding the birds, she walked around to the front of her house. With slow measured steps she walked down the dirt road to her mailbox to collect the Union Tribune. Maggie did not read the front page of the paper. She set that aside, preferring to read the local news, the comics, and the obituaries. She brought the paper back to the deck, poured herself another cup of coffee, and began to read. Beginning with the front page of the local section, she skimmed a short article about a Fallbrook man who had been charged with distributing Fentanyl. A second article on the same page related the sad tale of a poor nineteen year old woman who stopped to help some people who had been in a car accident, and was hit by a passing SUV. She didn't survive. Hoping for something a little less depressing, but doubting that she would actually find it, Maggie unfolded the newspaper. She skimmed the opinion section on B7. Today's debate was on the pros and cons of police surveillance.

"Can police really surveil the population without a warrant or probable cause and enter the information into giant data bases?" Maggie wondered. Looking for something a bit lighter she turned back several pages.

On page B2 she saw an article about the house explosion in Carlsbad. This was interesting. She scanned it quickly. The owner had been inside and was deceased. His name was listed as Dr. Michael Carmichael, and his age as 67. He had worked for a company called Quantum Computing Dynamics as an engineer of some type. The cause of the explosion was listed as gas leak.

"What?" Maggie thought. She was sure she had seen the drone fly into the window of the house. "Why was there no mention of the drone?" Maggie replayed the scene from yesterday in her mind. Yes, she was sure that the drone had flown directly into the window. She felt she should tell someone about what she had seen, but whom? Walking inside, she pulled out an old phone book for North County. Flipping to the government section, she located the number for the Carlsbad Sheriff Department, non emergency calls, pulled out her old flip phone, and dialed. When she was finally connected to a human, after a seemingly unending series of computer generated prompts, she explained that she had information about the explosion that could be important.

"You can make a report online." The person told her.

"I don't have internet access." Said Maggie.

"Then you will have to come in and make a report in person." They explained. "Ask for Detective Truesdale when you arrive." Maggie ended the call and folded her phone. She returned to her bedroom and stood in front of the mirror. Looking into her own green eyes she had a silent conversation with herself.

"What would Ed do?" She asked herself, already knowing the answer.

She pulled on faded jeans, a new t-shirt and her ball cap, grabbed her wallet and keys, and with another deep sigh, headed out the door and back toward Carlsbad.

11

A.I. SMITH

S mith's real time tracking of Dolores' car indicated she was up and moving. A drone on standby behind a bush near her home was activated and began transmitting images to Smith. Hacking into Dolores' car's computer was not difficult for Smith. Pulling up a map of the area, Smith located her car heading South on El Camino Real. The large and very busy intersection with La Costa Avenue was a mile in front of Dolores. Smith took control of the vehicle and accelerated. Sensors indicated that Dolores had the brake pressed to the floor, but it was fruitless. Smith was in control. If Dolores had thought to look, she would have noticed the drone that had been hovering over her since the moment she backed out of her driveway. Through the footage provided in real time through this drone, Smith was able to steer Dolores' car straight into the base of the stoplight at a high rate of speed. Smith heard no sound from the footage of the car smashing head on into the post, but through the drone was able to see the devastation caused by the crash. Glass and twisted pieces of metal flew into the air. The front was demolished, pushed back into the body of the car. Smith had disabled the air bags and was confident Dolores could not have survived the accident, but would monitor the frequencies of the first responders to be sure.

12

ELSIE

The gentle vibrating of her phone woke Elsie from a deep and dreamless sleep. Retrieving her phone from beneath her pillow, she saw a text from Phil received 1 minute ago, and that there was a missed call and voicemail from Dolores. She had obviously slept through that call, which had come over an hour ago. Elsie sat up, reached her arms above her head for a long stretch, and checked the text message first.

Hey babe, sorry I didn't check in last night. Lots of calls. U were at the lagoon? It was a gas explosion. Guy died. Pretty messy. Going for a run.

He included a smiley face and a heart which made Elsie smile. Phil was a good guy. They had been dating since March, sleeping together since April. Not serious yet, but definitely had potential.

. . .

Next Elsie turned her attention to the voicemail.

"Elsie, God, you never answer your phone. Jeannie is dead! Her house cleaner found her on the kitchen floor this morning. I can't believe this. I'm on my way to the hospital now. I'm her doctor, I might be able to get more information. I just can't believe this, call me."

Elsie was stunned. Jeannie dead? They were all together yesterday. Elsie liked Jeannie. She had been the one to teach Jeannie to paddle board the previous year. Unlike Maggie, Jeannie had been open about the loss she was dealing with. Her daughter, an only child, had died of cancer, and her son-in-law had taken the two young grandchildren and moved to Idaho. Jeannie was in contact regularly by phone and internet, but was struggling with loneliness and depression. She seemed to have been making progress. "How did she die?" Elsie wondered.

She tapped Dolores' number and listened as the phone went straight to voicemail. "Dolores, call me." Elsie said and disconnected.

Feeling the need to get out of the house, Elsie decided to take a run. She pulled her long, auburn hair into a ponytail and applied sunscreen to her pale face and neck. She dressed in shorts, a tank top, and running shoes. Phone in hand and music flowing through her earbuds she exited her driveway, turned right, and took off towards Fire Mountain Road.

An hour later, panting and sweaty, Elsie rounded the last corner before her home. At that same moment two CHP cars rounded the corner, passed her, and parked in front of the driveway she shared with the Campbells. Removing her earbuds, and picking up her pace, she neared the driveway just as the officers were stepping out of their cars. One was a man, hard to tell his age with the sunglasses on, about 5'10", with close cropped dark hair. The second was a woman, white blonde hair pulled into a tight pony tail, and standing about the same height as Elsie. The woman paused when she saw Elsie approaching. "Do you live here?" she asked.

"Yep, I rent the guest house from the Campbells. Did something happen to one of their kids?"

"We are looking for Elsie Davenport." She replied. "Do you know her?"

"I'm Elsie. What's up?"

The officer removed her sunglasses, revealing large brown eyes that reminded Elsie of a kindly bovine. "Can we talk to you inside?"

"Am I in some kind of trouble?" Elsie asked.

"No, we just need to talk to you, can we come inside?"

Reluctantly, Elsie led them past the Campbell's garage and into her small rental.

"I'm Sergeant Calabrese and this is officer Jensen, our police chaplain." said the male officer. "Are you the daughter of Dolores Davenport?" He had removed his glasses and Elsie guessed him to be in his mid forties. His expression was hard to read.

"Yes, is she ok? I tried to call her a while ago but it went straight to voicemail. Her friend died today. Is this about Jeannie?" Elsie stopped, realizing she was rambling. The chaplain suggested that Elsie sit on the couch, which she did.

"Your mother was killed in a car accident this morning. I'm

so sorry to be delivering this news to you." Sergeant Calabrese said.

The words hit Elsie like a physical blow. She felt their impact in her gut.

"No, I mean I just saw her yesterday, she left me a message this morning, I heard her voice, she was fine....Where, who hit her, she's a careful driver, she has a new car, it should have protected her." The words poured out of Elsie's mouth unbidden. "This can't be true, it can't be happening. Where is she? I want to see her."

Officer Jensen stepped forward as if to put her arm around Elsie. Elsie flinched and backed away. "Don't touch me." The chaplain took a step back.

Sergeant Calabrese said "Do you have anyone else who lives here with you? Is there someone we can call to come be with you?"

"I live alone. My boyfriend, Phil. I'll text him." She grabbed her phone and sent a quick message. *I need your help. Can you come over?* His affirmative response arrived seconds later. "He's on his way. He lives close. What happened? Was it a drunk driver, or someone texting?" Elsie's eyes were welling up as she thought about Dolores. She blinked rapidly, and felt a few stray tears trickle down her cheeks.

"According to multiple witnesses your mom's vehicle struck a steel light post at a very high rate of speed." Said Sergeant Calabrese. Elsie was silent.

"Has your mom been suffering from depression recently?" Elsie eyes grew wide, yet she still did not speak.

"How far away does your boyfriend live?"

The answer came as the screen door slammed and Phil rushed in.

"Elsie, what's going on?" He crossed immediately to Elsie, gathering her in his arms.

"They just told me Dolores is dead." She whimpered. "Make them go away."

Phil asked the officers to repeat what they had told Elsie. He listened, saying nothing until the end. He then asked for information regarding the case number, where the car had been towed, and where Dolores' body was being held. When he had all the information he thanked them for their time and showed them out the door. Returning to Elsie, he pulled her close to his chest and held her while she cried.

13

DETECTIVE TRUESDALE

Detective Loyal Truesdale leaned back in his chair and put his feet on his desk. His stomach rumbled, and he glanced at the clock on the office wall. 10:00 AM. He had been at the station all night, and was scheduled to go home in an hour. It had been a busy night and he was hungry and tired. All his reports were finished and submitted. Loyal remembered the old days when reports were actually written with pen and paper. He disliked filing reports electronically, and still took notes on a notepad, transferring the information onto the computer when he found the time. He ran his hands through his shaggy light brown hair and looked with dismay at the buttons straining across his belly. His formerly loose Tommy Bahamas were fitting snugly these days. What had Stella said when they last met for lunch? He looked like an former athlete gone to seed. She was brutally honest, and yet he smiled at the thought of his only child, a product of his first failed marriage. She was right, he had let himself go after the demise of his second marriage several years ago. Fast food and beer, too much of each.

. . .

Loyal looked out the narrow window of his office and saw a yellow dune buggy pulling into the parking lot. A woman wearing a baseball cap slid out of the car, took a moment to look around, and headed towards the department's lobby door.

"Oh God, I hope she's not here to see me." Loyal thought.

There was no way he would get out of here by 11:00 if she was. Several minutes later Loyal's desk phone rang. "Detective Truesdale." He answered. He listened a moment. "I'll be down in a minute," he said as he hung up the phone. "Damn." He muttered under his breath. The lady was here to make a report. The officer at the front desk had said that she was claiming to have information about the explosion by Carlsbad Lagoon. Truesdale heaved himself out of the chair, grabbed his notepad and pen, and lumbered out of the office.

When he turned the corner into the reception area, the first thing Truesdale noticed was the woman's long black hair and trim figure. Her back was to him as she examined photos and notices on the walls.

"Ahem." He cleared his throat and approached her. She turned at the sound. He guessed her to be a few years younger than himself. Big green eyes watched him from beneath the lid of the stained ball cap she was wearing. He took in details about her, the fine lines around her eyes and mouth, the casual clothing, and a brittleness he sensed rather than saw.

"I'm Detective Truesdale. How can I help you?"

Her voice was surprisingly low. "I have information about the explosion yesterday by the lagoon. I was paddle boarding that morning. I saw it."

"Alright, let's start with your name, then you can tell me what you saw." He said.

"Do we need to go to an office?" The woman asked.

"If it is fine with you we can talk right here." Loyal motioned around the empty reception area.

"I'm Maggie Macphearson." She spelled her last name for him. "I saw a drone over the water yesterday. It flew into the big window in the front of a house, and then the house exploded."

"Good looking, but bat shit crazy." Thought Truesdale, flipping to a clean page of his notepad. Out loud he said "Let's go back to the beginning and you tell me everything you saw."

She paused a moment, then said "I was paddle boarding with my therapist, well actually with my therapist's daughter. It was my first time and Dolores had other clients there too. They were faster than I was, so they were pretty far ahead."

Truesdale interrupted, "How about if I walk you through it with some questions. When did you first notice the drone?"

"We were just going under the freeway. I remember because Elsie said something about the noise."

"The 5 freeway?" Truesdale asked. "That puts you pretty far away from the house. Do you wear prescription glasses?"

"I know what I saw." Maggie replied.

"Ok, walk me through it."

Maggie paused, focused her green eyes on him for a moment, and then slowly told him how the drone had flown over the water and headed straight to the house. When the drone hit the window the house exploded. "I didn't see anything for a minute or two after that. The explosion disrupted my balance and I had to drop to my knees. Elsie saw everything though. You should talk to her. Elsie Davenport, I don't know her number."

"That's easy enough to locate." Truesdale replied, making a note of Elsie's name on his note pad. "Do you know who was piloting the drone?" He asked. He was wondering if he could locate the drone operator. He didn't believe for a minute that the drone had actually caused the explosion, but maybe there was footage he could review.

"How would I know that?" Maggie retorted.

He recorded her phone number, noted the information she provided, thanked her and turned away saying "I'll be in touch if I need anything else from you." Maggie looked at the business card he had handed her, let out a deep sigh, and walked away.

"Might get out of here on time after all." Thought Truesdale as he walked back to his office.

14

MAGGIE

"Loyal Truesdale, great detective he is." Maggie thought sarcastically as she slid back into her buggy and headed for El Camino Real. Her limited experience with cops was that they were overly confident and already had their minds made up before they even had heard the facts. Detective Truesdale appeared to be no different. Probably a few years from retirement, just counting the days. Eating out too much too, from the look of it.

"I'll be in touch." He had said. Sure. He hadn't cared about anything she had told him. Maggie didn't deny that it could have been a gas explosion. That was possible, but could it have been caused by the drone? She was more sure than ever that the drone had something to do with it. The ringing of her phone interrupted Maggie's thoughts. No way to answer her phone in the buggy. Between the engine noise and the wind rushing past it was difficult to even hear the radio. Maggie figured if it is important enough they would leave a message. She would check when she was safely back in Valley Center. She turned the volume dial on the ancient radio to the right and sang along with Green Day's <u>Boulevard of Broken Dreams</u> as she drove home.

45 minutes later Maggie parked the buggy in the driveway and went into the house. She hadn't changed a thing since Ed's death. It was always slightly surprising to her that he wasn't here somewhere. She eyed his record player on an end table, his records stacked beneath it. All the good oldies. She hadn't played one since he died. It wasn't even noon yet and the day stretched out before her like a giant chasm. When Ed had been alive, it had felt as if there were never enough hours in a day, now the days seemed like they would never end. Sighing, Maggie picked up a framed picture that sat on the coffee table. She and Ed, squinting into the afternoon sun, a breeze ruffling their hair. The buggy was in the background. This picture had been taken on one of their many trips to Borrego. They both loved the desert, especially at night. She recalled Ed struggling to set the self timer for this particular picture. He had set the camera on a large rock and run back to her side. They had wrapped their arms around each other and smiled.

"We were so happy."

Maggie forced herself to set the picture back down on the table. She was living in the past. She was aware of this, her tendency to lose herself in her memories. She liked it better in the past, with Ed. Dolores had told her that this was not healthy. She could have her memories and still live in the present, Dolores said. Maggie was undecided on this point.

Searching for a distraction, she remembered her phone ringing while she was driving. Retrieving the phone from the car, she sat down to listen to the voicemail.

"Hello Mrs. Macphearson, its Patty from Dr. Davenport's office." Poor woman sounds sick Maggie thought. "I'm calling to inform you that Dr. Davenport was killed in a car accident this morning. I'm very sorry to have to deliver this news. Our office can recommend some other psychologists to you. Please call if you have any questions or concerns."

The voicemail ended yet Maggie just stood there, still holding the phone to her ear, as if she were waiting for Patty to laugh and tell her this was all a big joke.

"Can this be true?" Maggie thought. Another loss, another person she cared about that she would never see again, another goodbye not spoken out loud. She tried to remember her flippant words when she left the lagoon yesterday. She hadn't even thanked Dolores. Her shoulders sagged forward. Life was too cruel. One moment the people you cared about were with you, then the next moment they were gone. Her thoughts moved to Elsie. She'd be devastated of course. There was never a good age to lose one's mother, Maggie knew this first hand. She'd have to support Elsie by going to the funeral. Maggie dialed Dolores' office number. When Patty answered Maggie asked about the funeral service. She was told that it would be held at 10 am Saturday. Patty recited the address of the church in Carlsbad and Maggie promised she would be there.

15

R ealizing she had not yet eaten, Maggie opened her well stocked fridge. She was aware that she still shopped for two. It was a habit she had been unable or unwilling to break. If she shopped for one was she denying some tiny portion of Ed's memory? Scanning the shelves, she decided that breakfast was more appealing than lunch. She chose a few vegetables, an egg, a jar of salsa, and some butter. Ten minutes later she was on the back deck with a vegetable scramble steaming on the plate in front of her. Maggie took small bites, chewing slowly. Her mind wandered back to Dolores. What an incredible loss her death was. The psychologist's uncanny ability to see through her client's barriers was something Maggie had discovered early on. She thought back to one of her earlier sessions, recalling Dolores' words.

Do you want to know what I see when I look at you Maggie? I see a woman adrift at sea. The waves are huge and relentless. In your boat you have a life vest, oars, flares, maybe even an outboard motor, but you refuse to use any of them. Instead you let the waves crash over you, again and again, threatening your very life. When are you going to start helping yourself survive? Put the life vest on, Maggie. Take a small step to save your own life.

Maggie put her fork down and gently massaged her temples. She had listened to Dolores, had taken her advice. That was the reason she had been on the lagoon in the first place.

"What am I going to do without Dolores?" She thought, then stopped. How incredibly selfish of her. "Poor Elsie must be suffering terribly." She thought. "I hope she finds a way to cope with her loss better than I have with mine." Rising, she carried her plate and fork into the kitchen, rinsed them and placed them in the dishwasher. She noticed, not for the first time since Ed's death, that it took forever to fill the washer up. She looked at the clock. 12:46. Exhaustion cloaked her like a heavy blanket. Recalling the digital clock this morning, Maggie realized that she had been up for over nine hours, and had gotten very little sleep the previous night. Perhaps a nap was in order.

Tracy Attkinson was proving to be a bit more difficult to track. She owned a smart phone, but had location services disabled. Images from early morning drone surveillance showed her car in the driveway and no apparent activity in the house on Lolita Street. Her car was a 2016, so the option for hacking the computer the next time Tracy ventured out was always a possibility. She did not work, and her medical files did not indicate any underlying health issues that could be manipulated like Jeannie Espinoza's peanut allergy.

Redirecting, Smith hacked into the medical files for Jeannie Espinoza, quickly changing the recorded cause of death from anaphylactic shock to heart attack. Logic suggested that a more common type of death would attract less attention. Smith scanned through reports from Hazmat officials and arson investigators regarding the explosion on Beachwood Court. So far nothing out of the ordinary was being reported. All signs pointed to a natural gas explosion, which in truth it had been. Smith had hacked Dr. Carmichael's natural gas smart thermostat and filled the house with gas. The spark from the drone was all it took to cause the explosion.

Satisfied, Smith focused again on the two heat signatures that had been detected in the shadows of the overpass yesterday morning. Even with video enhancement Smith could not identify the two individuals. Shadows were difficult for Smith. The logical argument was that the two people beneath the overpass were somehow connected to the three visible in the lagoon. Smith searched another database and found that the funeral for Dolores Davenport had been scheduled for Saturday morning. Drone surveillance of those attending would be advisable. In moments Smith had assigned two drones the task of facial imaging all attendees.

Smith had access to the most innovative software available, which made it possible for multiple processes to happen simultaneously. While the drone tasks were being programmed, the computer in Tracy Attkinson's car indicated it has been started and was being driven. Smith pulled up a map and located the car in real time. She was heading North on Coast Highway 101. When she turned East on Leucadia Boulevard Smith saw the opportunity. The crossing signal gates that prevented motorists from crossing the railroad tracks as the coaster commuter train sped through Leucadia had just been lowered. An elevated percentage of accidents were already associated with this particular crossing. Tracy's computer indicated that she had stopped at the gates. Smith raised the barrier in front of Tracy. The car's computer indicated forward movement, then abrupt stopping. This was because Smith had raised a single barrier, which was now lowered, effectively trapping Tracy and her car on the tracks. At the same moment, Smith engaged the car's locks, ensuring that Tracy was prevented from escaping. In less than a minute Smith's ever present scan of local first responders showed several 911 calls reporting an accident on the tracks. Smith would, of course, continue scanning, but was 100% sure it was unnecessary. A vehicle, when broadsided by a train traveling at 94 mph, would produce no survivors.

Maggie's nap lasted for nearly an hour. She awoke groggy and confused. "What day was it? Had she imagined Dolores' death?" She sat up on the couch, trying to focus. Dolores had died, she remembered that now. There had been a car accident. Maggie picked up the picture from the coffee table again. She looked into Ed's eyes, felt the warmth from them, felt his love for her. In therapy sessions, Maggie was beginning to confront her feelings of guilt regarding Ed's death. Dolores had been steadily drawing Maggie's feelings out, feelings that were excruciatingly painful. She closed her eyes, leaned back on the couch, picture still in her hands, and recalled the devastating day.

"Ed, are you coming or not? The sun sets in less than an hour. We have to leave right now. I want to get these pictures." Maggie said. She was gathering her camera bag, tripod, wallet, and keys. "Ed? Are you coming with me?"

"I don't think so Maggie, I'm feeling kind of sick. I think I'll just stay here and play ham radio with the guys . Do you mind?"

Maggie smiled, and gave him a quick kiss. "Nope. Tell everyone 7 3's. I'll be back in a few hours. Love you."

The door closed on Ed's echo of "I love you too."

The sunset had been spectacular. The view west from the Palomar Mountain outlook was one of the best. On clear evenings like this she could see all the way to the ocean. Maggie took hundreds of shots. She would go through them tomorrow and delete the shots she didn't like. She had driven home in the dark, smiling at her success.

Maggie knew something was wrong the moment she approached her home. No outside lights were shining. Ed always turned lights on if Maggie was arriving home after dark. Perhaps he was sleeping, she thought. As she pulled into the driveway Maggie noticed something on the ground. Pulling closer so the headlights illuminated it, she realized it was Ed. Pulling on the brake and leaping from the buggy she ran to his motionless form. "Ed! Ed!" She yelled, rolling him from his position on his side to his back. Maggie pulled the flip phone from her pocket, dialed 911, then set it on the asphalt as she began CPR. She heard the operators tinny voice and screamed out loudly "My husband isn't responding, I need help!" She yelled out their address and continued CPR. "Ed, please, breathe! Please, please, please!" Maggie had not turned off the buggy, and the headlights shone brightly on her as she struggled to revive her husband. She could see her teardrops, scattered across his chest and soaking into his shirt. Sirens screamed in the distance, coming closer. Never once did she stop CPR. Her arms and back were aching, but she would never abandon Ed. The air-cooled buggy, overheating, coughed and turned off. The headlights dimmed, barely illuminating Maggie and Ed. Moments later the ambulance and fire truck arrived.

Blinking back tears, Maggie brought herself back to the present. Of course she felt guilty. She had gone off to take sunset pictures and left him alone. That fact was the hardest for her to deal with. He had been alone. The cause of death was a massive heart attack. Maggie would never know if she could have saved him had she been there. This was the question Dolores had been helping her to deal with. Helping her understand that no one could change what had happened. Maggie had to forgive herself, let the question go, and move forward.

I t was Thursday afternoon and Loyal was on the phone. Larry, his friend and an industrial accident investigator, was working the site of the explosion at Beachwood Court.

"Larry, I'm just wondering, off the record, if you have found anything unusual."

"Everything looks pretty normal Loyal. Definitely a natural gas explosion. Guy might have had a leak overnight and set it off with a spark somehow in the morning. I'll keep digging. Oh, one thing we did find were some commercial drone parts. It wasn't registered with the FAA, so I don't know if it belonged to Carmichael or not."

Loyal could here Larry rustling through his notes.

"Here it is, the brand and model is dji Matrice 600 Pro. Has a capability for carrying 5 cameras. Can send footage in real time through telemetry. Costs around $5000."

"Drone parts?" Loyal thought. The crazy dune buggy lady had mentioned drones.

"Where were the drone parts in relation to the house, Larry?"

"They were near the large glass window in the front of the

house. We found a few glass fragments embedded in the drone pieces."

"Appreciate it Larry, let me know if you find anything else." Said Loyal, hanging up the phone.

Loyal leaned back in his chair and rubbed his right hand along his jaw. He turned to his computer and did a quick image search for the Matrice 600 Pro. The thing was a beast, over six feet wide, and twenty pounds. Resembled a giant mosquito. Loyal recalled his comment to the buggy lady -what was her name again- about prescription glasses. That had pissed her off. Maybe this was why. A drone this big could easily have been seen from the underpass.

A You Tube video comparing drone noise gave Loyal an idea of the sound it would have made. She would definitely have heard the thing. Damn, he was going to have to interview her again. Loyal still did not think the drone caused the explosion, but he was thorough, and this was an angle he had to investigate. He pulled out his notepad and turned to the page with her details. Maggie Macphearson. He had her phone number and her address in Valley Center. Loyal dialed her number and listened as it rang. Eventually he heard the generic computerized voice announce that the phone subscriber was unavailable. Loyal left his name and number, along with a message asking her to please call him as soon as possible.

M aggie slept until 5:45 on Friday morning. Thankfully, she didn't remember any dreams. She followed her usual routine of coffee on the deck, and walking to the mailbox for the daily paper. Settling in on the deck with her second cup of coffee, Maggie opened the local section and began to read. Woman Dies in Train Accident, read the headline. "Not again," thought Maggie. The next sentence stopped her short. *Tracy Attkinson of Leucadia was killed instantly when her car was broadsided by a train.* "Tracy Attkinson?" Thought Maggie." That sounds familiar." It took a moment for Maggie to make the connection, but when she did she was shocked. Tracy was one of the other clients that had been paddle boarding on Tuesday. The introduction in the aftermath of the explosion had been brief, but Maggie was sure this had been the woman's name. She read the short article again. Not much information was provided, just that Tracy had been stuck on the tracks and hit by the train.

Maggie considered the odds. Dolores killed in an unexplained car accident, and now Tracy too? Maggie did not believe in coincidences, and this would be a huge one. She considered the fact of the drone. What had it been doing over the lagoon at that early hour. Who had been piloting it? She was sure it had hit the window, and that created the fact of another suspicious death. What was going on? Should she call the authorities? Maggie looked around for her phone, she was always forgetting about it. When had she last seen it? She thought back. She had used it to call Dolores' office on Wednesday. She hadn't used it at all yesterday. She stepped inside and checked the coffee table. There it was, next to the picture of herself and Ed. Maggie picked it up, then froze. Who should she call? Unsure, she flipped it open and saw that she had a voicemail. Listening, she heard Detective Truesdale's voice and his message for her to call him.

"How will he react when I tell him about Tracy," she wondered. "He already doesn't believe me about the drone." Maggie thought for a moment. She decided that rather than calling Truesdale, she would check in with Ed's ham radio friends. He used to talk to those guys all the time about a wide variety of topics. She was wondering about drones, and who used them. The drone she had seen had been fairly large. The ham radio guys seemed like a good source of information. She headed to Ed's radio room, anxious to hear what they would have to say.

Maggie keyed up. "Hey guys, anyone out there? It's WW6RV, Maggie." She listened for a moment, hoping that some of Ed's friends were out there this morning. When talking on ham radio she used the Astronomy Club's call sign instead of her own. She was a member of the club, so this was acceptable. She didn't like to use her actual call sign now that she lived alone. People could look up call signs online and access all kinds of information. Maggie did not need any more trouble.

"Hey Maggie. Good to hear you out here." YPA came back at her. "It's been a while."

"Yep, sorry Dave, I've definitely been quiet. Good to hear your voice."

"Hi Maggie, Dave. How are you guys?" The new voice belonged to HDX. Within minutes a few more guys, KHV, BME, and AZQ had joined them on the repeater.

"I was wondering what you guys can tell me about drones." Maggie said. She and Ed had talked with these guys for years. They did not fit the stereotype of ham radio operators, fat guys eating Cheetos and living in their parent's basements. Maggie knew that they were an intelligent and well educated group. They loved to talk about gizmos and gadgets. She figured if anyone was going to know about drones it would be these guys.

Conversation flowed back and forth, and soon Maggie had learned that, judging by its size, the drone she had seen was likely a commercial drone. Many groups and agencies used drones such as these. Everything from Hollywood, to park rangers, to scientists, to the CIA. Maggie needed to narrow it down, so she asked a more pointed question.

"Can drones cause a natural gas explosion?" she asked. This question sparked multiple return questions from the repeater user base. Maggie gave them a quick run down of the events of the last few days. Listening to herself talk, she had to admit it all sounded pretty wild. The guys seemed to agree with that assessment and immediately launched into conspiracy theories and ideas about rogue agencies.

"You know, drone technology is very advanced. All kinds of

military and government agencies use them. NSA, CIA, FBI, and probably some with acronyms that we aren't even aware of." Said YPA.

"I just saw a YouTube about micro drones." Added KHV. "These things are crazy scary. The militarized ones can be programmed to take out a single person or a whole city. And they are autonomous, so no one is guiding them. The operator just programs them and then the drones make their own decisions."

AZQ added "And the car accident, that could have been hacking. These newer cars, its like we are driving damn computers."

"I don't like the sound of this Maggie." Said YPA. "If I were you I'd get out of town for little while."

"I agree that someone could have hacked their cars." Said KHV. "You still driving the buggy? That's a safe bet, no computer, no way to hack it."

Maggie assured everyone that she was safe, and still driving the buggy. She thanked the guys for the information and suggestions, and promised to be better about keeping in touch. She set the mike down with a shaking hand, wondering what she had inadvertently gotten herself involved in.

Maggie spent the remainder of the day puttering around the house, and pondering her situation. She did not return Detective Truesdale's call. If her radio friends were even remotely correct about an agency being involved in the explosion and car crashes, then it stood to reason that contacting a member of a police agency was not the smartest thing to do. She promised herself that she would contact him on Monday, after she had gotten through the funeral and had time to think everything through.

Elsie was adrift. Once, over a rare shared bottle of wine, Dolores had told her how the metaphor of being adrift at sea fit nearly every one. "I love my clients Elsie." She had said. "I want to help them recover the part of themselves that they have lost. But they all truly just need to learn to help themselves. The metaphor helps."

"How can you use the same lines with everyone? That feels like cheating."

"It opens them up. Grief is a universal emotion. Most people experience it in similar ways."

Elsie was experiencing it now. Thursday and Friday had been a blur. Thank God for Phil, with her every moment, helping with everything. Dolores was a planner, and in her safety deposit box Elsie had found a receipt for a pre purchased plot in a cemetery. This solved the question of where to bury her. Elsie asked the office staff to help her notify everyone on Dolores' contact list about the accident and her death. This left coordinating with the funeral home, contacting the cemetery, and planning the reception. Additionally, she needed to collect photos of Dolores to display, order flowers, and plan for food. Phil, thinking of everything, had reminded her to decide what she was going to wear and make sure it was ready on the day of the service.

Elsie looked at her reflection in the oval full length mirror. Also reflected in the mirror was the pile of clothes on her bed and Phil, sitting on the couch in the living room. She saw him check his watch again. Elsie unclenched her jaw and rolled her shoulders. She looked in the mirror again, turned to the pile on the bed, grabbed a royal blue dress, and pulled it over her bra and underwear. She slipped her feet into a pair of low slung black heels.

"Ready." She said as she walked toward the door. Phil stood and followed her out, wisely choosing not to mention his advice about choosing her outfit in advance.

The funeral was being held at a Presbyterian Church. Dolores had pre purchased her plot, but she had not specified a location for the service. Neither Elsie nor Dolores had any religious affiliation, so when Elsie had noticed a church across the street from the cemetery she had stopped in and inquired about holding a service there. The pastor had agreed to perform the service in the church's chapel.

Elsie and Phil arrived about 20 minutes prior to the starting time. They spoke briefly with the pastor, confirming small details, then headed into the chapel. Bouquets of flowers filled the small room, perfuming the air. Dolores had been loved by so many. Soon the chapel was full of mourners and small whispered conversations swirled through the air. Everyone quieted as music began to play. When the song ended the pastor spoke a few words then introduced Elsie. She spoke of Dolores' passion for her clients, and of her own love for her mother. After Elsie, a few friends spoke about Dolores, the pastor led them in a short prayer, and the mourners filed out of the chapel.

21

MAGGIE

Maggie sat in the very back of the chapel during the funeral service. She had slept fitfully the previous night, and was feeling brittle and edgy today.

She had arrived at the church a bit early, and chosen to park on the street for a quick get away. By the time she had parked and walked back people were already heading into the chapel. She had followed an older couple in, they were sweetly holding hands, and picked a spot in the very back.

The pastor said a few words, and then introduced Elsie. She looked so pale and fragile. How well Maggie knew that pain. Elsie was composed and spoke lovingly of Dolores. After Elsie, a few other people spoke and the pastor closed with a prayer.

Maggie waited for everyone to exit before she stood and walked into the narthex. Eyes down, she headed towards the back door and a quick exit. She was looking down at her feet when she heard the sound. A humming, like a blowdryer or small fan. Maggie walked to the front door and peeked out, looking up. Drones, two of them, were circling overhead. Heart hammering, she pulled her head quickly back inside the narthex. She turned towards the back door, then thought of Elsie. She risked a peek back out front and saw her, just to the left of the door, in quiet conversation with an older couple.

"Elsie" she called quietly. Elsie turned at the sound of her name and spotted Maggie. She said something to the couple, gave each a quick hug, and walked into the narthex.

"Hi Maggie. Thanks for coming."

Maggie grabbed Elsie's arm and pulled her close.

"Do you hear that?" She whispered.

"Hear what?" Elsie asked.

"There are two drones out there." Maggie said.

Elsie started towards the front door saying "I didn't notice them."

Maggie stepped quickly up to Elsie grasping her upper arm. "Don't go out there."

Elsie's eyes slid down to Maggie's hand on her arm, then back up to Maggie's panicked green eyes.

"I've learned some things since the explosion Elsie. We aren't safe here. We need to go right now."

"I can't leave Maggie. Dolores' service isn't over."

Maggie propelled Elsie towards the back door.

"I'll explain on the way. Please trust me Elsie."

Elsie looked at Maggie then back towards the front door. Maggie was pulling harder now.

"Please Elsie, let's go." Elsie allowed herself to be pushed through the back door and down the street towards the buggy. The women's heels slapped the pavement as they ran.

Confused and frightened by Maggie's words, Elsie allowed herself to be led through the back door and ran with Maggie towards the yellow buggy. Maggie slid in the driver's side, dropping her keys in the footwell. By the time she had retrieved them Elsie was in and fastening her seatbelt.

"Can I see your phone?" Maggie said. Elsie handed it to her. The buggy lurched forward and Maggie tossed Elsie's phone over her shoulder and into the street.

"Wait, Stop!" Elsie yelled. She struggled to remove her seatbelt and turned to face backwards, knees on the seat.

"Stop Maggie, my phone!" She screamed. Elsie turned to look at Maggie. "Stop or I'm jumping out." she yelled. Maggie turned to Elsie, a grim look on her face, and removed her own flip phone from the side pocket of the buggy. She opened it, broke it in half, and threw it out of the car.

"Go ahead and jump." She said.

"You are crazy." Said Elsie as she reluctantly turned and sat back in her seat. She wasn't going to jump out of a moving vehicle. She turned back one more time and saw Phil standing in the street staring after them.

Elsie looked at Maggie. "What is going on?"

"I'm pretty sure some agency is killing everyone who was on the water Tuesday. I know it sounds crazy but the guy in the house is dead. Dolores is dead, and Tracy is dead."

"Tracy is dead?" Said Elsie. "Jeannie is dead too."

"What?" Said Maggie. "How?"

"Her maid found her on the kitchen floor Wednesday morning. I think she had a heart attack or something. What happened to Tracy?"

"Her car was hit by a train." Said Maggie.

"Oh my God." Said Elsie. "I can't believe this."

"Believe it." Said Maggie. "We aren't safe. We need to get out of here. I know a safe place we can go."

"I still don't get why you threw our phones away."

"Whatever agency it is, they obviously have access to all kinds of technology. Our phones can be tracked. They had to go."

23

A.I. SMITH

The unidentified heat signatures were a detail that Smith was focused on. Two drones had been dispatched at the end of Dolores' service, and were scanning faces into the facial recognition software. Smith worked quickly and efficiently, examining information on each attendee and analyzing the probability that any of these people could have been on the water that day. Two files were created, possibilities and impossibilities. Analysis of text messages between Elsie and Dolores had confirmed that Elsie was on the water that day. The second person was as yet still unidentified.

Movement on the back side of the narthex was detected and Smith directed one drone to fly that direction. The video footage showed a yellow vehicle in the distance and a man standing in the street with something in his hand. Zooming in, Smith saw that he held a cracked smart phone.

DETECTIVE TRUESDALE

W alking down the hall past the radio room with a fresh cup of coffee, Loyal overheard a 911 call coming in. A kidnapping was being reported. The caller, one Phil Gillespie, was stating that his girlfriend had just been kidnapped from her mother's funeral. The description of the vehicle was "yellow dune buggy".

Loyal moved quickly. He leaned into his captain's office. "I'm following the marked unit on this one Captain. I might know who this suspect is." He said. Loyal checked that he had his notepad and pen, grabbed the keys and hurried out the door.

He arrived at the scene a few minutes after the marked unit. Parking his car on the street, he joined the patrol officers. They were talking to a dark haired man in a suit.

"I need to interrupt guys." Loyal said to the patrol officers. Turning to the dark haired man he said "I'm Detective Truesdale." Loyal pulled his notepad and pen from his pocket. "What's going on here?"

"I think my girlfriend, Elsie Davenport, was just taken

against her will. I saw Elsie and a dark haired woman run out of the chapel and get in a dune buggy. Then the dark haired lady, who was driving, threw Elsie's phone out." He was holding the cracked phone in his hand.

"I need to know who was driving that buggy." Loyal said.

Phil said "You might try asking Dolores' receptionist. I think a lot of her clients are here today."

"Who is Dolores?" Loyal asked.

"She is, or was, Elsie's mom. This is her funeral."

"Can you direct me to the receptionist?" Loyal asked. Phil pointed across the street. "She's speaking at the grave site."

"I'd like to talk to her. These two officers will take your full statement." Loyal said as he turned to cross the street.

Loyal stayed toward the back of the crowd, keeping an eye on the squat dark haired woman who had spoken at the graveside. She seemed to know everyone, and was working her way through the crowd dispensing hugs. She spoke to nearly every person. Loyal supposed that she was offering kind words and sympathy. When he saw her nearing the edge of the crowd he approached.

"Hello, I'm Detective Loyal Truesdale of the Carlsbad Sheriff Department. Can I have a word please?"

"Um, sure, I suppose so. Is it ok, I mean, am I supposed to ask to see ID?" she said.

He showed his badge, and asked her to move a bit away from the group.

"Are you Dolores' receptionist?" He asked.

"Yes I am. My name is Patty Larson. What's this about?"

"I'm looking for information about a woman who drives a yellow buggy. I was told you might know her." Loyal said.

"Is she ok?" Asked Patty.

"Yes, I just wanted to confirm that I have the correct information." Said Loyal, pulling out his notepad. He flipped to the page where he had recorded Maggie's information. He read the name he had written down, Maggie Macphearson.

"Yes, that's her. I can't really give you any more information, you know, patient confidentiality and all." Said Patty.

"I just need to know if she's acquainted with Dolores' daughter, Elsie."

"Well, I guess I can help with that. Elsie taught Maggie to paddle board last Tuesday. I think it was the first time they met." She leaned in close to the detective. "Just between you and me, I think it is pretty strange that of the five women who paddle boarded that day, three are dead."

Maggie insisted that they stop at her house and get some cash, supplies, and change their clothes. "I always keep some cash hidden." She told Elsie. "In case of emergency, and I think this qualifies."

Elsie nodded, but remained silent. She sat, turned slightly away from Maggie, and stared out of the car as Maggie drove. They passed through the edges of Escondido, and drove up a short grade to Valley Center. Elsie had heard of the small town, but had never been here. It didn't look like much to her. One road ran through what she thought was the town; two lanes in each direction. There was a giant gas station, a few low profile farm supply stores and a market. Surprisingly, there was a golf course on the right and large houses dotted the hills surrounding the valley.

Maggie turned left off the main road and drove along quiet back roads. It was midday and the sun beat down with a vengeance. The buggy had no roof; Elsie felt small drops of sweat dripping down her back. There were oak trees all around. Many looked to

Elsie as if they were dying, their bare branches reaching towards the sky like twisted arthritic fingers. Few provided any shade over the road.

Maggie turned at a single mailbox, and steered the buggy onto a narrow dirt road. About a football field's distance in front of her, Elsie could see a ranch type house at the end of the road. The house was simple. Stucco walls and tile roof. A few healthy oak trees shaded the garage, which was separated from the house by a covered walkway. Maggie parked and slid out. "Come on in." She said to Elsie over her shoulder.

Elsie walked into the entry way and then to the living room. She sat on the couch and picked up the picture on the coffee table. Maggie and a man squinted back at her. The wind was blowing their hair and they were smiling. The yellow buggy was in the background. Maggie looked like a completely different woman. In the picture she was vibrant, alive. She looked so happy. The woman she could hear rummaging around in the other room was colder, more brittle, angry. "Well, I guess this answers the question of who she lost." She thought, setting the picture back down.

Elsie stood and looked around the room. The living room and dining area were open to each other, allowing both rooms to be seen at once. The furniture and decor was simple, the house felt comfortable and lived in. There was the aging brown leather couch upon which Elsie had previously been sitting. The glass topped coffee table, fashioned from half an oak barrel held up by an iron framework held the picture of Maggie and the man. A round wooden dining room table and four wooden chairs occupied the dining room. The living room also housed a pot belly stove, a bookcase packed with books, and an end table. A closer look at the books revealed a fine layer of dust settled upon them.

"Ok, now lets just check in with Peter and make sure he has room for us." Maggie said as she passed behind Elsie and headed through a door into another room.

Elsie looked around the living room again. Something was off. She spent a moment surveying the room. Then it clicked, there weren't any electronics in the room. No TV, no computer, not even a router that Elsie could see. Just an old record player on the end table, and some records stacked beneath. "How does she function?" Thought Elsie. She walked over to the stack of albums. The Beatles, Elton John, Journey, all old bands. Nothing current. Everything in this place was from the past. Elsie paused at that thought. Maybe there was a land line here somewhere. She could call Phil and have him come get her. She did a quick search of the kitchen and found nothing. She glanced at the door Maggie had gone through, it was still closed, and walked quickly down the hall. She checked what she assumed was Maggie's room, nothing. A quick look behind the other two closed doors revealed an office and a guest bedroom. Both were dusty and unused, and neither had a phone.

Elsie took a deep breath, attempting to calm her pounding heart. How had she allowed herself to be taken by Maggie? No one could possibly be after them. This was all Maggie's crazy imagination. "Ok," she told herself. "Think this through, Elsie. You need to get to a phone or computer. Obviously that isn't going to happen here. You just need to hang on until we get somewhere that you can make a call or send a text or email. Wherever we are going is sure to have a phone." Feeling better now that she had a plan, Elsie turned and entered the room Maggie was in.

"What the...?" Elsie took a breath and stopped herself from saying anything more. The room was packed full of equipment. There was a table stacked full of black boxes. The boxes had multiple dials and gauges; there were wires coming out of everything. It looked like the instrument panel of an airplane, or perhaps something you would find in a submarine. Hand held radios leaned haphazardly against the boxes. Maggie was seated in a chair and speaking into some type of microphone. A few of the radios on the table looked like the radios she had seen when visiting Phil at the fire station.

"So it's ok if we come stay for a while?" Maggie was saying. A man's voice answerd, "Sure, come on out. Stay as long as you want."

"Copy that Peter, WW6RV." Said Maggie. "See you in a few hours. And thanks again."

Maggie turned to face Elsie. "Peter lives in Borrego. He's pretty much off the grid. It's a good place to disappear for a while."

"What is this room?" Said Elsie.

"It's the radio room." Replied Maggie. "All the radios serve different purposes." She pointed to one of the larger ones. "This is a 10 meter transceiver. With it I can talk to New York in the morning, and in the evening I can talk to my friends in Australia."

"Why don't you just use the phone or e mail?" Asked Elsie. "This seems so archaic."

Maggie set the microphone down. "Well, we don't have phones at the moment, do we? Come on, let's get moving."

"Oh my God," thought Elsie. "I've actually managed to offend her again."

As she walked out of the room, Maggie turned and said "We need to change clothes." She disappeared into her bedroom and returned, handing Elsie some shorts and a shirt. "You can borrow these. I don't think my shoes will fit you. What size do you wear?"

"Eight." Elsie said.

"I'm a six. Wear the shoes you have on for now. We can get you something in Borrego."

In the bathroom, Elsie slipped on the long sleeved shirt and baggy shorts. "Ugh, old lady clothes." Still wearing the low heels she wore to the funeral, Elsie walked out to the buggy and saw that Maggie had changed into a similar outfit. Her black ball cap was on her head and she was wrestling a small duffel into the space behind the passenger seat.

"Great, we look like twins." Elsie thought as she slid into the buggy.

Maggie started driving down the dirt road, then stopped and reached behind her seat. She pulled out a faded brown ball cap and handed it to Elsie. "You're pale, you're going to need this." she said. "Take good care of it, it was Ed's."

26

L oyal sat on the sand and looked out at the lagoon. There were a few kayakers on the water, and one person riding a jet ski. He took his notepad out of his pocket and studied his notes, which were woefully thin. A seemingly crazy, and hard to locate, woman had started everything. The yellow dune buggy driver was the key to this case, if it could even be called a case. It was more an assortment of facts that didn't quite add up. After Patty's admission that Elsie and Maggie were acquainted, there had been no choice but to have the boyfriend, Phil, wait to see if Elsie contacted him. She wasn't technically missing if she drove away with an acquaintance. Phil had made his opinion about this known, loudly.

"If anything happens to her because you waited on this you are going to regret it." He had said. Loyal had let the threat go. Heck, the kid was upset.

He tried to come up with a basic timeline in his mind. The house explosion had been Tuesday morning. When the body was discovered in the house, Loyal had decided to hang around the station, waiting to see if the investigators suspected foul play. That had turned into an all nighter for him when there had been a gang shooting at a nearby park. He had been tired and cranky when Maggie had shown up. He hadn't given her another thought until Larry reported the drone parts near the front window of the house. According to Patty, Dolores' receptionist, there had been five women on the water that morning. Three were now dead, and two were missing. Taken separately, two car accidents and a heart attack were not unusual. But taken in the context of their proximity to the exploding house, the three deaths were, in fact, very unusual.

"I really need to find the buggy lady." Loyal thought. He stood and brushed the sand off his pants. He had her address, he might as well start there.

It took Loyal almost two hours to reach Valley Center. Traffic on the 78 freeway had been gridlocked, and there was roadwork going on at the base of the grade to Valley Center where two lanes were narrowed to one. Loyal could remember a time when there had been virtually no traffic at all. He thought, not for the first time, that relocating out of California might be a good idea when he retired. The only thing keeping him in the state once he retired was Stella. He turned on to Maggie's dirt road and parked in front of her house. Loyal could tell before he even got out of his car that she wasn't home. Still, he exited his Altima, and went through the motions of looking for her. He knocked on her front door, announcing himself loudly, and got no response. He walked around the house, peeking in windows, even tried a side door. He was able to make his way completely around the house, and found nothing. He did pause for a moment on the giant deck built off the back of the house. Huge rough hewn beams held up a massive wooden roof. A wooden table and two deck chairs faced a line of eucalyptus trees. "Hell of a view." Loyal thought. He could picture her sitting here, sun rising behind her at dawn or setting in front of her at dusk. "Where are you?" he whispered.

27

She didn't want to admit it, but Elsie was enjoying riding in the buggy. Pulling her hair into a ponytail and lowering the cap on her forehead, she settled into her seat. The road was a two lane and the buggy was climbing in elevation. The last sign they passed had read 3500 feet. Huge oak trees lined the road. The sky above them was blue, but in the East Elsie could see some giant puffy clouds, white at the top and gray toward the bottom.

"If we are lucky we might get some sprinkles on the way out." Maggie said loudly over the clattering of the engine and the whistling of the wind. "Those are towering cumulus clouds. You will appreciate their shadows once we are closer to the desert. It's only going to get hotter."

Elsie nodded at her. She could feel the heat on her skin already and was grateful for the hat that shaded her face.

The road leveled off and they passed an obviously shrinking lake on the left. Maggie braked suddenly and hard. "Shit" came out of Elsie's mouth before she could stop it.

"Sorry, but look." Said Maggie. Elsie looked where Maggie

was pointing, and smiled. Crossing the road in front of the buggy was a line of wild turkeys. Two hens, one in front, one in back, three babies in between them.

"That's so cool." Said Elsie.

"You have to be careful along this stretch of road." Said Maggie. "These little guys cross it a lot."

Elsie felt an unexpected prick of sadness as she watched the little family gather together on the other side of the road. She began sifting through her memories, searching for one that would show Dolores in that nurturing, protective light. Somehow it was always Laurene who showed up in her mind's eye. Laurene, who Dolores had hired to live with them and take care of Elsie after her Dad moved away. Steady solid Laurene. It was Laurene who drove Elsie to all her lessons. Laurene who helped with homework, made dinner, played games and bandaged knees. When Elsie had her tonsils out in seventh grade Laurene slept on an air mattress in Elsie's bedroom for two nights in case she needed anything. When Elsie thought of a nurturing person in her life she thought of Laurene.

Elsie liked to compare people to animals and had always thought of Laurene as a St. Bernard. She was a big woman, cuddly and soft. Protective too. She always had Elsie's back, even if Elsie was wrong. Of course they would talk about it later, but in front of anyone else Laurene was always on Elsie's side. Dolores' animal twin had been harder to pin down. Dolores was elegant, graceful, charming and intelligent. She was a strong woman who's opinion was nearly impossible to change. She had, of course, been a part of Elsie's adolescence. She was present, yet at the same time not really there. Ephemeral. In her freshman year of high school Elsie had finally decided on a unicorn. A magical, mystical creature that one wanted to believe was real, but no solid proof could be found. Later, as an adult, Elsie had been amused to learn that unicorn was also slang for a woman who would consent to join a heterosexual couple for a threesome. The joke being that this was a mythical creature who didn't actually exist.

Elsie had been waiting for the right time to share that last bit with Dolores. She glanced to her left, studied Maggie's profile briefly, and wondered what jokes from her life with her husband remained unshared.

They turned left at a stop sign and continued along another two lane road. Elsie found the lack of other vehicles strange. In Oceanside traffic was constant. Being out here, in what felt like the wilderness, would have been a great adventure if the circumstances had been different. She wondered what Phil was thinking, how confused he must be. She still couldn't believe she had just left without saying anything to him. When she had turned in the buggy, right after Maggie threw her phone out, he had been standing in the street watching them drive away. She would contact him as soon as they got to Borrego.

The oak trees slowly gave way to dry fields. Elsie saw a herd of cows on her right. They stood together in small clumps and nibbled on the grasses at their feet. Huge rock piles were peppered throughout the fields. Trees, some dead and some alive, were scattered about as well. The clouds, which reminded Elsie of enormous piles of shaving cream, appeared massive as the buggy got closer to them. She could see the vertical movement at their peaks. The wind came at the buggy sideways, battering their faces and tossing tumbleweeds, which Maggie smoothly avoided, into their path.

Maggie turned left, and Elsie read the sign on the side of the road out loud."Ranchita 5 miles".

28

A.I. SMITH

Smith enhanced the image of the yellow car that had sped away from the funeral, then began searching images from stoplight cameras in the general area. It didn't take long to locate the yellow vehicle. Smith tracked it's progress, although not in real time. The car drove East on El Norte Parkway in Escondido. It was recorded passing through the intersection of Bear Valley Parkway and Lake Wohlford Road. The last image showed the vehicle turning left off Valley Center Road on to Lilac.

Smith was easily able to identify the two people in the vehicle. Maggie Macphearson and Elsie Davenport. The two heat signatures identified at last. Massive amounts of information were available about Elsie Davenport. Smith had already analyzed this data. Maggie Macphearson, however, had much lower Internet exhaust. Smith had her address in Valley Center, which made the fact that there were no more stoplight images of the yellow car logical. She did not have an Internet connection at her home, and the car she drove had no computer. This would make elimination more difficult, but not impossible.

· · ·

Smith put taps on both ladies' phones. Taps were also placed on the phones of Phil Gillespie and Detective Loyal Truesdale. The identities of the men were ascertained though analysis of Elsie and Maggie's phone records. Alerts were put on credit cards for these same four individuals. Smith hacked into the Detective's office computer, requesting a general be *on the lookout* for Maggie's yellow dune buggy. Smith would wait for something to pop up. Until then, there was still much work to finish before the mission was complete.

Maggie spotted the approaching vehicle in the distance at the same time as she heard Elsie read the sign for Ranchita out loud. As it neared she saw that it was a sheriff. He slowed a bit, and looked over at them as he passed by. She kept an eye on him in the rearview mirror, and saw him brake and execute a u turn when he was about two football fields away. "Dammit."

"What?" Said Elsie.

Maggie didn't respond, just downshifted and turned quickly on to a narrow dirt road. A small white sign identified it as Grapevine Canyon. The buggy bounced as she drove quickly down the bumpy road. In the rear view she could see the sheriff turning on the dirt road behind them, lights flashing and siren blaring. Elsie looked over her shoulder, then at Maggie.

"Pull over." She yelled at Maggie. "You have to stop for him."

"No way." Said Maggie, focusing intently on the rough road. "It's going to get too narrow and rocky for him pretty soon."

"You are crazy, you can't run away from the police. At least stop and let me out."

"No." Said Maggie.

"We haven't done anything wrong. Just stop to see what he wants."

"No." Maggie repeated. She glanced in the rearview and saw that the sheriff had stopped his forward motion.

"He will just call for back up, Maggie, you can't out run the police."

"We are in the largest state park in our entire nation." Said Maggie. "And there are only three rangers. There isn't back up."

Picking up the radio in the buggy, Maggie said "Peter, you out there?"

He replied a moment later. "Copy Maggie."

"I'm going to need you to come meet us on Grapevine. Bring your biggest tarp and some tie downs. Meet by our favorite tree in about 40 minutes."

Peter asked no questions, just agreed to the request, and signed off.

"I don't want to do this Maggie." Said Elsie. "I just want to go home and forget about everything. I don't believe your theories about us being in danger, and I'm done playing your crazy games."

"This stuff is real." Said Maggie. "You saw the drone too, Elsie. I don't believe it is a coincidence that Dolores, Tracy, and Jeannie all died within 24 hours of the explosion. That drone dipped down and looked at them, you saw that."

Elsie sat still, eyes focused on the vast desert.

"Privacy is an illusion." Said Maggie. "The phones, the cameras everywhere, social media, we are being tracked all the time. I read articles in the newspaper every day about ethics and technology. Did you know that in China the government has drones that look like birds and are equipped with cameras? They monitor their citizens."

"That is China." Said Elsie. "We are in the United States. We have protections against that kind of stuff."

"Don't bet on it. I'm sure our government does the same kind of things. And then there is private industry as well. Who is monitoring them? You know what privacy is Elsie? It is this, us, here in the desert. No cameras, no phones, no computers. Who knows our actual location? No one. Only you and me."

L ooking into Stella's expectant brown eyes, Loyal bit into the sandwich and chewed thoughtfully.

"Well?" Asked Stella.

"It's pretty good. Tastes like chicken." Said Loyal.

"Right? But it's not, that's what makes it so great." Said Stella.

They were having dinner at a small vegan restaurant in Encinitas called Plant Power. The main offerings were hamburgers and chicken sandwiches, both of which were made using no meat products.

"Are you vegan now?" Loyal asked.

"No, but this is a healthier version of something you already like. I felt it was my duty to introduce you to it."

Loyal smiled at his daughter, glad that she had called and suggested meeting for dinner. He told her about his search for "the buggy lady" as he had come to refer to Maggie. Stella took out her phone and tapped it a few times, then turned it so the screen was facing her father.

"Is this what the dune buggy looks like?"

"Yep." He said. "Pretty much, except hers is yellow, and I think it has two seats, not four."

"Maybe she's a member of a car club or something." Suggested Stella. "Seems like people with unusual cars like to join clubs." She had turned the screen back toward herself and was tapping again. "Says here there is a Manx Club. They have groups all over the world, but the club is based out of Valley Center. Isn't that where you were this afternoon?"

Loyal popped the last bite of his sandwich into his mouth and chewed. Swallowing, he said "Yep, I was. Can you send the information on the club to me? That could definitely be a good avenue of investigation. You're pretty clever, sure you don't want to be a cop?"

"Hell no," laughed Stella. "I've got my hands full teaching hormonal seventh graders math."

"I don't know how you handle that Stella. I'll take criminals over seventh graders any day of the week."

"Is the lady you are looking for a criminal Dad?"

"I don't think so. She's more like a puzzle piece, a big one, and I can't see the whole picture without her."

The absence of law enforcement chasing them, coupled with her lack of desire for conversation with Maggie, created an opportunity for Elsie to take in the beauty of the desert. Grapevine Canyon Road was a single lane sandwash. There were chatter bumps, ruts, and rocks to maneuver over and around. The buggy was traveling about 15 to 20 miles per hour. Elsie narrowed her eyes and pictured the lines she would take if she were on her bike. She would certainly be going faster. With four wheels rather than two, the buggy necessarily traveled more slowly. Inhaling deeply, Elsie discovered that the desert, like the coast, had its own unique scent. Sage brush lined the narrow lane, filling the air with its pungent fragrance. Despite the humidity, the air smelled dry. Enormous gray and white clouds floated above them casting occasional shadows which, like giant umbrellas, cooled her skin. One thing was certain, the desert was hot.

The rain came suddenly and with great fury. Giant drops fell from the sky, beating down upon their exposed bodies. Lightning flashed, thunder boomed. Neither woman spoke. Maggie focused on the rough terrain, coaxing the buggy over large slippery rocks and through deep ruts that ran with rain water. Elsie sat, hat off, face to the sky, allowing the huge drops to pelt her face. The drops were fat and stung her skin, but she didn't mind. The experience was worth it.

The rain stopped as suddenly as it began. The shadows previously cast by clouds disappeared, and the temperature rose quickly. Elsie felt the burning heat on her thighs.

"My skin can't take much more of this." She said.

"We are almost there. Two or three more curves in the road. We are past the hard rocky part, mostly smooth sandy washes from here." Maggie said.

They rounded a curve and Maggie stopped the buggy. Directly in front of them was a magnificent tree. A long gray trunk shot up from the sand. About ten feet up giant branches grew in all directions. Green leaves were vibrant against the now blue sky and barren desert. Behind the tree and slightly to the right was a row of willow trees. Despite her frustration at Maggie, Elsie couldn't help but comment on it's beauty.

"Amazing." She said.

"Our favorite tree." Maggie said. "An underground stream keeps it alive."

She eased the buggy past the tree and nearer to the willows, cutting the engine and engaging the parking brake. Elsie turned at a rumbling noise behind them, and saw an old rust colored jeep with a soft top approaching. Maggie was out of the buggy and running towards the jeep before it had completely stopped. An older man, tall with thick gray hair and wearing tan shorts, white shirt, and hiking boots, stepped out of the jeep. Elsie noticed the rectangular radio clipped to his belt. Disembodied voices emanated from it. The man swept Maggie up in a bear hug. He was extremely tan, and his white teeth glowed in his leathery face. The hug was brief, but fierce. Releasing her, he reached into the jeep and produced the requested tarp and tie downs.

"You'll need to get out of the dune buggy Elsie." Maggie said. Elsie quickly unstrapped and slid out. She stumbled as her heels sank in the soft sand making walking difficult. Maggie grabbed the duffle and threw it in the jeep. She and the old man covered the buggy with the tarp and secured it with the tie downs.

"I hate to leave her here, but don't see any other option." Said Maggie with a sigh.

"Don't worry Maggie, no one is coming out here this time of year, she'll be fine." Said the man. He turned to look at Elsie, stuck out his hand, and said "I'm Peter. Pleased to meet you."

She shook his hand and introduced herself.

"Hop in the jeep and let's get you ladies home. I've got a great dinner waiting for you."

"It will take about ten minutes to reach the paved road." Peter said to Elsie over his shoulder. Elsie noticed that the jeep was a much rougher ride than the dune buggy had been. They reached the paved road and Peter waited to execute his left turn as a sheriff car passed. The sheriff was driving slowly, his head swiveling as he scanned the desert. Maggie looked over her shoulder at Elsie. Neither said a word. Peter pulled out behind the sheriff and followed the slow moving vehicle toward Borrego.

Ahead of them the sheriff signaled, then pulled into a campground parking lot on the right. The jeep continued on. The road angled upward, rising in elevation. They drove up a series of switchbacks. With each sharp turn more of the desert below was revealed to Elsie. Her heart sank as the jeep wound upward. The land around her was desolate and barren. The rocky jutting hills appeared to have risen straight up from the desert floor. After a last sharp turn they crested the hill. The valley lay spread out below them. Peter slowed and pointed to his left and slightly behind them.

"See all the channels leading down from the mountain into the desert basin?" He said. "That is called an alluvial fan. They are predominantly found in deserts. When we get a rare rainstorm the water flows down those channels to the desert floor."

Normally Elsie would be interested in information like this as she loved geography. Today, however, as she looked at the large expansive basin, she felt an even deeper sinking feeling in her stomach. There wasn't much to the town, at least not from up here. It looked like scattered houses and desert. "Where is the city?" she asked.

"This is it." Said Peter. "Welcome to Borrego."

The town of Borrego may have been a disappointment to Elsie but Peter's house was not. It sat alone, surrounded by a wrought iron fence. Cactus, palm trees and other desert plants Elsie could not name surrounded it. Peter drove the jeep through large wrought iron gates and pulled up to the front. The house was large, made of adobe bricks that had been painted white, and had a red tile roof. They entered through a massive wooden door. Elsie was struck by the beauty of the living room. The floor was made of reddish brown Mexican pavers. A huge Persian rug fronted the fireplace, with three tan leather couches arranged upon it in such a way as to facilitate conversation. The room was a rectangle, long with a low ceiling containing huge wooden beams. Windows dominated three of the four walls, letting in natural light that illuminated the artwork on the walls. The air was cool.

"I'll show you your bedroom Elsie." Said Peter. "Maggie knows where her room is." He led her down a long narrow hallway, pointing out the bathroom on the right, and then opened a door on the left. They entered a room nearly as large as the living room. It had the same adobe walls, Mexican pavers and low ceiling with wooden beams. The bed was enormous, with a giant pale leather headboard and fluffy white pillows. Windows lined one wall, allowing natural light to fill the room. A small couch sat in one corner.

"Is this the master bedroom?" Said Elsie. "I can't take your room Peter."

"No, this is a guest room. The house is quite large, my room is on the other end. Set your things down and come join us for dinner."

"If you don't mind, I'd rather just lay down and rest. It has been an exhausting day. Oh, and I was wondering if I can use your phone?"

"I don't have a phone. I communicate with my ham radio, or go to the airport in town if I need to make a call." Peter said.

"Can I use your computer to send an email?"

"Don't have that either. If you want to make a call we'll have to wait until tomorrow and use the phone at the airport."

Elsie's hands and feet twitched as she dreamt, much in the same way that a puppy's paws did as it dreamt of chasing rabbits across an open sunlit field. Elsie was not dreaming of rabbits. She was on a paddle board on Carlsbad Lagoon. Surprisingly, Dolores floated beside her. The water was still, the sun gentle. Dolores looked at Elsie; smiled. As always Elsie was struck by Dolores' beauty. Flawless skin, honey colored hair, light green eyes with a darker green rim around the iris, straight white teeth.

"I have something to say to you Elsie." Dolores said.

"Ok."

"It has been a long time coming." Dolores said.

"I'm listening."

"I'm not one for apologizing Elsie." Dolores said. "You know that. But I feel I owe you one. I'm sorry for.."

A bright flash of lighting and loud crack of thunder drowned out Dolores' words. In an instant the sky had turned dark. The water was choppy. Balancing was tricky. Elsie saw that Dolores was struggling to stay upright. She tried to paddle closer to her mother, but the board and paddle did not obey her commands.

. . .

As Elsie watched helplessly, Dolores fell off her board and was sucked under the angry waves. She reappeared for a brief moment, then went under again. Elsie searched the water for signs of Dolores. There! She could see Dolores again, about fifteen feet in front of her, struggling in the rough water. Elsie tried to call out to Dolores but words would not form on her uncooperative lips. She was paddling furiously, digging deep, but was getting nowhere. Her hands and shoulders ached with the effort. Ahead of her Dolores went under, reemerging a moment later, clearly weakening.

Elsie bent deep at the knees and forced the paddle deeply into the water. Instantly she realized she had overextended. The board tipped too far to the right and instantly Elsie was under water. She struggled against the angry waves, disoriented and unsure which way was up. *So this is how it ends,* she thought. She stopped her frantic battle, relaxed her muscles, and closed her eyes. It was in this moment that she realized something had changed. The consistency of the water was different. She opened her eyes. The water surrounding her was no longer angry and black. She was floating in a sea of silvery-gray. It was cool and soothing. Looking up, she saw the roiling water above her. She inhaled impulsively and found, curiously, that she could breathe. She began moving, swimming slowly, searching for Dolores. Surely her mother could breathe in the water as well. Ahead of her Elsie saw a giant kelp forest, the fronds swaying in the gentle current. She swam in, gently moving the leaves aside so she could pass through. It was magical. She reached her right hand out to move a large frond aside and out popped Dolores. She was dead, her face frozen in a silent scream, small fish nibbling on her nose and cheeks. Elsie recoiled and jolted awake.

She sat up, gasping. "What the hell?" She stood up and turned to look at the bed accusingly, as if it had the power to cause such nightmares.

"Think good thoughts Elsie," she told herself pulling the extra large t-shirt Peter had loaned her more tightly to her trembling body. "Think happy things." In an attempt to banish the image of Dolores' tortured face, Elsie looked around the large guest bedroom. A row of cowboy boots lined the narrow shelf below the windows. Looking more closely, Elsie saw that Peter had cleverly tucked a rolled up magazine inside each boot. The room had no clock, but the mystical quality of the light coming through the slats in the window blinds suggested pre dawn. "Five-thirty-ish?" Elsie guessed.

The dream image of Dolores still clear in her mind, Elsie exited the bedroom and wandered down the long hallway to the living room. Peter owned many paintings. They were hung on the walls in such a way that the natural light illuminated them. She studied one. Three Indians on horseback carrying spears. Two upright, one whose horse has fallen, flinging the rider to the ground. A herd of buffalo to the left and behind the horsemen. In another three horses ran across a grassy field; puffy white clouds and blue sky above them, dancing green grass below. The skull of a cow hung on the wall to the left of the fireplace. Horseshoes were placed here and there, their appearance haphazard, although Elsie suspected strategic placement. Cowboy hats hung from a hat stand near the front door. The thick Persian rug beneath her feet was certainly authentic. An oak corner bookcase was filled with books. Mostly hardbacks, Elsie noticed, with a few paperbacks thrown in. She ran her hands lightly along their spotless spines. "When was the last time I read a book?" She wondered. "College?"

Elsie thought about Maggie and Peter, considered their lifestyles, their lack of connectivity. She felt as if she had traveled through time; in the wrong direction. Half a smile formed briefly on her lips at that thought. She wandered out of the living room and into the large kitchen, grabbed a water bottle from the industrial sized fridge, and stood at the large kitchen window. A kidney shaped pool nestled among brown Mexican pavers was directly outside. Its blue water sparkled, reflecting the early morning light. Beyond the pool, and Peter's fence line, lay the desert. Miles and miles of sandy earth dotted with green scrub brush. In the distance mountains rose proudly from the desert floor. She would take a picture if she had her phone.

Elsie understood that she belonged to a unique generation. She was a child before the advent of cell phones for the average person. How well she remembered the land line in their home. Pay phones, too, once dotted the civilian landscape. She was thirteen when she received her first cell phone. The stick phone was a gift from Dolores. It made phone calls. The next year she had received a flip phone that had texting capability as well. Each number key stood for two or three letters. She and her friends used to have contests to see who could text the fastest. Then came the smart phone; and exponential growth of its capabilities. Elsie had been untethered for the first thirteen years of her life; tethered the next fourteen.

· · ·

Elsie left the kitchen intending to walk through the dining room and back to the guest room. A painting hanging in an arched alcove stopped her short. It was a portrait. In it a woman sat, holding a child in her arms; a girl. Both woman and child gazed directly out of the painting, almost as if they had spied Elsie at the exact moment she had spied them. A half smile was formed on the woman's lips. She looked content. Judging by the flowing clothing and the woman's head covering it was likely representative of the Renaissance time period. Elsie had taken an art history class in college. She enjoyed it so much she had considered changing her major from Environmental Studies to Art History. Dolores had vetoed that immediately. The one class was all Elsie took. It covered art history in very broad strokes. Elsie stared at the painting. She thought about Dolores, and their stiff, slightly formal relationship. She had always blamed Dolores for this. Looking back now, she realized that she, too, held some of the blame.

Elsie shook her head. She wasn't used to quiet time, to reflection. She found she really didn't like it. What was the point of revisiting old hurts and disappointments. She missed her electronic distractions. With a last glance at the woman and child, she walked down the hall and back to the guest bedroom. She would try for a few more hours sleep. When she woke she would go in search of a phone.

34

S unday morning found Loyal sitting at his home computer in his one bedroom apartment on Roosevelt Street. He wore faded gray cotton boxer shorts and a tattered green t shirt. Steam rose from the mug of black coffee in his left hand. Through the magic of Google he had learned that the buggy lady drove a Meyers Manx dune buggy. The club was founded by Bruce and Winnie Meyers of Valley Center. Google images had provided hundreds of pictures of the couple, always with a buggy near them, in all kinds of exotic locales. Loyal liked the look of the couple. Unpretentious, usually in jeans, always smiling, Bruce was an older guy with fly away white hair, twinkling blue eyes, and an engaging smile. Winnie appeared to be a bit younger than Bruce, with short blond hair and pleasant features. Loyal watched a You Tube interview featuring Bruce discussing the history of racing in Baja. Seemed the guy was an off road legend. Bruce had started the Mexican 1000, which became the Baja 1000, the most grueling and televised off road race in the world. Together, Bruce and Winnie had started the Meyers Manx corporation. Bruce was the artist and visionary, while Winnie managed the day to day operations. Loyal did not normally look forward to interviews; meeting the Meyers was sure to be a treat.

Changing into jeans and a Tommy Bahama, Loyal made the drive up to Valley Center. He found the Meyers' home at the end of a long dirt road and parked in the circular driveway. To his left was a stand of palm trees. To his right he saw a Spanish style house with arched entryways and palapas on the adjacent patio.The house was white stucco with a red tile roof. There was a small office next to the house. A World War Two quonset hut containing buggies in various stages of assembly stood open next to the office. Loyal got out of the Altima just as the door to the house opened and a woman who he recognized as Winnie stepped out to greet him.

"Can I help you with something?" She said.

"I'm Detective Truesdale from the Carlsbad Sheriff Department. I was hoping to speak with Bruce and Winnie Meyers." Loyal said flashing his badge.

"I'm Winnie, what's this about?"

"Is Bruce home?" Asked Loyal. "I was hoping to speak to you together."

"Wait here," said Winnie as she turned and walked back to the house. "I'll get him and we can talk in the office," she said over her shoulder.

Loyal waited, and soon Winnie and Bruce walked back out. She unlocked the door to the office and all three crowded into the space. It was full of memorabilia. Posters and pictures of Bruce covered the walls. Two tiny desks, each with a computer and land line, were covered in knick knacks representing Bruce's storied career. Winnie pointed out a folding canvas chair. "Have a seat." She said.

. . .

Loyal removed his note pad and pen from his shirt pocket and stuffed his bulk into the chair, hoping it wouldn't collapse. "I'm Detective Truesdale." Loyal said to Bruce. "I appreciate you two giving me a few minutes of your time. I'm trying to locate Maggie Macphearson. She drives a dune buggy, and I thought perhaps she might be a member of your buggy club."

"Is she in some kind of trouble?" Winnie asked, confirming to Loyal that Maggie was indeed a member.

"Not at all. She came to see me at the station on Tuesday. She had seen something that didn't seem right to her. I just have a few follow up questions. She's not at her home, and she doesn't answer her phone."

"I can try to call her for you, she usually answers for me." Said Winnie, pulling an old rolodex toward her and flipping through it. "She's notorious for not answering her phone."

"How long have you known Maggie?" Loyal asked Bruce while Winnie was preoccupied.

"I'd guess about 15 years or so." Said Bruce. "She and Ed came to a few runs before they decided to build their own buggy."

"Straight to voicemail." Said Winnie, hanging up the phone.

"Who is Ed?" Loyal directed his question to Bruce.

"I don't think we need to..." began Winnie, but Bruce cut her off.

"Ed was Maggie's husband. He died, what was it Winnie, about a year ago?"

"Yes, a little over a year." Said Winnie.

"He had a heart attack. It was such a tragedy. We all really enjoyed Ed." Said Bruce."

"Yes, he was such a nice man." Said Winnie. "It has been hard for all of us, but especially Maggie."

"Do they have any children?" Loyal asked. He picked up a business card from Winnie's desk, flipping it absently from front to back and returning it to the plastic card holder.

"Nope, it was just them." Said Bruce.

"Do you have any idea where Maggie might go if she wanted to get away for a few days?" Asked Loyal.

He noticed the cautioning glance Winnie gave Bruce.

"Probably Mike's Sky Ranch, it's in Baja." Bruce said.

"Damn it." Thought Loyal. "How far down is it located?" He asked.

"Deep in Baja. About 9 hours past the border, no paved roads. She loves it there."

"Do you have their phone number?" Asked Loyal.

"They don't have a phone. There's a number in Tijuana you can call for reservations, but I wouldn't bother with that. Maggie and Mike are great friends. She wouldn't need a reservation." Said Bruce."If you want to check and see if she's there you will have to drive down." Bruce glanced out the window at Loyal's Altima. "You'll never make it in that though." He paused a moment as if considering his next words carefully.

"You give me your word that this is in Maggie's best interest?"

"I do." Said Loyal.

"Ok, you want to go, we have a buggy you can use."

Loyal thought about this. His captain would have a fit if he traveled to Mexico. And Maggie might not even be there. It could be a huge waste of time. Still, he was at a dead end until he spoke with her again. Making a decision, Loyal said "Can you show me the buggy?"

Bruce smiled and stood. "Come on, I'll give you a tour of the place. You can borrow the French buggy."

"They manufacture the buggies in France?" Loyal asked.

Winnie chuckled. "No, only here. The French buggy is

owned by our friends who live in France. They keep it here for when they visit and allow us to loan it out."

"Do you know how to drive stick?" Bruce asked.

"Yes, it has been a long time, but I guess it is something you never forget," Loyal said as he followed them out of the office.

Bruce was a terrific tour guide. He showed Loyal *Old Red*. This was the original buggy he built, then drove in Baja, in 1964. Loyal listened, interested, as Bruce explained the process of building a buggy from a kit that he and Winnie produced and sold. The kit fit best on pre 1974 Volkswagen bugs. Bruce had a guy that would put it all together for the customer, but his hope was always that the building of the buggy be a project that brought a family closer.

"I've seen terrible rifts in families mended." Bruce said. "Often between father and son. Working together on a project like this can restore a relationship."

At last Bruce presented the buggy he would loan to Loyal. It was lime green, faded, and not nearly as bright as Maggie's. It had two seats and no roof.

Half an hour later, looking in the rear view and grinding second gear as he drove away, Loyal could see Bruce standing in the driveway watching him go. He couldn't be positive, but it looked to him like Bruce was laughing.

M aggie's phone had rung several times, always going to voicemail. No messages had been left for her until the one that came on Sunday afternoon.

Maggie, its Winnie. A sheriff's detective named Truesdale was here this morning asking questions about you. Says he needs more information from you about something you reported on Tuesday. Bruce suggested he go to Mike's to look for you, so he's borrowing the French Buggy and driving down there. Please call and let us know that you are ok.

Smith checked Truesdale's work computer again and found no notes or reports about anything that Winnie had mentioned. Smith hacked into the border patrol's system and searched for the yellow buggy crossing the border. There were no hits. It was possible that she had switched cars at her home, perhaps was even driving one that was not registered to her. She had few known associates, but Smith checked possibilities and found that no vehicles registered to anyone associated with Maggie had crossed the border either. If Maggie was in Mexico tracking her would be difficult. Satellites could be adjusted slightly to look at specific places, but not for long periods of time without discovery. The best course of action seemed to be to let Truesdale search for her down there.

Starting in Valley Center and radiating outward, Smith accessed all public cameras and began searching for Maggie, Elsie, or the buggy. The Pacific Ocean was a minor problem. Smith put watches on all cruises and charters leaving the Southern California coast. If they decided to go by ocean they would be found.

E lsie woke up and looked around, unsure for a moment where she was. Then she remembered. She was in Borrego with Maggie and Peter. Last night had been disappointing to say the least. Elsie had refused Peter's offer of dinner, choosing instead to go straight to the guest bedroom he had made ready for her. The horrific nightmare had woken her and prompted her pre dawn wandering. Her mission today was to find a phone.

Peter had already stated that he didn't have a phone or Internet. Elsie wondered what he did all day without any technology. Maggie would take exception to that statement, Elsie knew. Maggie would mention the ham radios, which Elsie was not sure fell into the category of technology. In Elsie's opinion Maggie's way of life was like living in the stone ages. Attempting to focus her thoughts, she recalled Peter mentioning a phone at the local airport. Her plan to call Phil was still a possibility. Surely Peter would drive her to the airport.

. . .

Elsie rose and walked to the window. The sun was definitely up now. She raised the blinds and placed her hand against the window pane, then instantly pulled away when she felt the heat. Damn, it was hot outside already. She slipped off the borrowed t-shirt and reluctantly re-dressed in the borrowed clothes from yesterday. After using the bathroom down the hall, she turned and entered the kitchen. The place was enormous. Stainless steel appliances gleamed in the reflected sunlight. A granite topped island sat in the center of the kitchen. A basket of fruit and a platter of scones lay in the center of the island, along with a thermal coffee dispenser. A note written in long slanting cursive instructed Maggie and Elsie to please help themselves. Orange juice and water were in the fridge.

Elsie grabbed a plate and loaded up. She opened the refrigerator for some orange juice, noticing with amusement that Peter kept his tea light candles on the bottom shelf. "How hot does it actually get out here?" She wondered as she walked into the dining room to eat. The scones were delicious, the crust flaky, clearly homemade. Elsie followed the scones with some strawberries and grapes then washed it all down with large gulps of orange juice. Satisfied, she sat back in the chair and pondered her situation.

Peter's whispered hello caused her to jump.

"Sorry, didn't mean to scare you. Just trying to be quiet so Maggie can sleep. I see you found the food. You were probably hungry after skipping dinner last night."

"Yes, the scones were delicious. Thank you." Said Elsie. Remembering her manners, she apologized for skipping the dinner.

"It's just that I don't want to be here, I want to go home." She said.

"Maggie seems to think you both are in some kind of danger. We didn't really talk much about it last night." Peter said.

"Yeah, she and I don't agree on that. I think she is over-reacting."

"How do you two know each other?" Peter asked.

"We don't really. My mom is...was her therapist. I just taught her how to paddle board. She grabbed me at my Mom's funeral, threw my phone out of the buggy, and dragged me out here. At one point the sheriff was trying to pull us over and she wouldn't even stop. Honestly, I don't get her at all."

"Maggie is complex." Peter said. "Come with me. I want to show you something.""

Peter led Elsie down the long hallway and into the huge living room. The desert sunlight poured in through the windows, illuminating the paintings she had studied just a few hours previously. They were even more beautiful in the bright light of day. He led her to the corner bookshelf. Reaching up, he retrieved something from the very top. He waved his large hand in the direction of the couches.

"Sit down Elsie." Said Peter. She chose a couch and sat. He sat beside her.

"I've known Maggie since the day she was born. Her Dad was my best friend. I can tell you lots of things about her, but this might help you to better understand her." He handed Elsie a tattered brown scrapbook and left the room.

E lsie opened the large book slowly. The first pictures were black and white, and showed a man, his arm around a pretty dark haired woman holding a bundle that Elsie assumed was a baby. Under the picture, in the same slanting cursive she had seen on the note this morning was the caption

Richard and Janey with Maggie January 2, 1963

The next picture was of a dark haired man, wearing a suit and tie, holding the same bundle. The caption read

Peter and Maggie January 2, 1963

She looked more closely at the man in the picture. Yes, she could see it now. It was a much younger Peter who held baby Maggie. He looked so proud. He could have been holding his own child.

Elsie turned pages and saw pictures of toddler Maggie, pictures of birthday parties and Christmas celebrations. The black and white turned to color, depicting Maggie's amazing childhood surrounded by two adoring parents and Peter.

"I don't know how this is supposed to help me understand her." Thought Elsie. "She had the perfect life." In one picture she saw that the mother was obviously pregnant again, and in another the family stood in front of a large two-story house holding a SOLD sign in front of them. The next page held a newspaper clipping rather than a photograph.

January 18, 1969

Six year old Margaret Atwood miraculously survived the mudslide that toppled her home on Mandeville Canyon Road yesterday morning. Killed were her parents Richard and Janey, and their unborn child. Brave Margaret managed to climb to the roof of the home and cling to the chimney until first responders could rescue her. Recent torrential rains have been the cause of massive flooding and mudslides in Glendora. Thirty-seven dead have been identified, with officials warning that the final count will likely be much higher.

Elsie read the short article twice, a strange feeling in her stomach. Everything changed in the pages that followed the article. The first picture showed young Maggie standing awkwardly next to a grim looking woman. Maggie held what looked to be a stuffed rabbit tightly to her chest. The caption said *Maggie and Aunt Joan*. Neither was smiling. There were yearly school pictures of an clearly unhappy Maggie. In some she was smiling, but the smile never reached her large green eyes. In the pictures of Maggie and Peter in the desert Elsie saw the happy Maggie. She and Peter obviously adored each other. Maggie jumping into the swimming pool, legs drawn up, arms reaching towards the sky. Maggie and Peter by a campfire, tent in the background. Maggie in the desert, high up on a ridge that the caption identified as Font's Point.

Elsie reached her hands behind her neck and pressed, then stretched, and continued looking through the scrapbook. Everything changed in the Summer of 1977. A skinny guy, with long, wavy, light brown hair and lively green eyes started showing up in pictures with Maggie. Elsie learned from the captions that his name was Ed. Maggie was smiling again. Pictures showed the two of them at the beach, at the mall, in the desert with Peter. There were pictures from high school dances, Maggie in her floor length floral gowns, Ed in a variety of pastel colored tuxedos.

In 1981 Ed graduated from high school, then Maggie a year later. Elsie saw their lovely wedding in the desert. Maggie in a simple white silk shift, Ed in a plain brown suit. Their eyes were bright, their smiles wide. The purchase of their new home was documented. Elsie recognized it as the home she saw yesterday. There was a picture of Ed holding a sign that read Macphearson's Electric. Elsie saw Maggie and Ed age together as she turned the pages. A love story unfolded in front of her. There were pictures of them building the dune buggy, then driving it everywhere. Sometimes just the two of them, sometimes a large group. They were always smiling. Elsie found herself smiling too, eagerly turning pages to see what their next adventure would be. Her smile faded as she turned the last page. Another newspaper article; Ed's obituary.

38

Maggie's stomach woke her. She had eaten little last night, picking at her food out of politeness. Peter had prepared stir fried rice with chicken and vegetables. His cooking was delicious, but her appetite had deserted her after the tense travels with Elsie. The girl was so rude. She had actually declined to sit at the table with them last night, going straight to bed instead.

Maggie rose, dressed in yesterday's clothes and went out to the kitchen. She read the note on the granite counter and piled some fruit and scones on a plate. She grabbed a bottle of Perrier from the fridge and walked towards the living room, stopping short when she spotted Elsie on the couch, her back towards Maggie. She backed up quietly and headed back through the kitchen and into the dining room. Choosing a chair facing a large window, she sat. She took a small bite of a scone and chewed slowly, savoring the flaky delicate texture. Outside the window she could see Peter's swimming pool, and beyond that miles and miles of desert. His house backed up to state property, guaranteeing the jaw dropping view would never change.

"Hey."

Maggie turned to see Elsie standing in the doorway. Her eyes were red and teary.

"I really want to go home, today, now." Elsie said.

"Did you eat?" Asked Maggie.

"Don't try to change the subject Maggie." Said Elsie. "I'm not kidding, I want to go home. You can't force me to stay here."

"We are both in danger..." began Maggie, but Elsie interrupted.

"No, we aren't. This is crazy."

"Well, I don't have a car so you will have to ask Peter to drive you." Said Maggie. "Check out front for his Jeep. Sunday is usually shopping day for him. I'm not sure he's even here."

"He was here an hour ago." Elsie said as she walked out, returning moments later. "The jeep is gone, but I'm not staying any longer. I'll walk to town if I have to. Someone, somewhere in this miserable little town has to have a damn phone."

Elsie pulled on her heels from the funeral and stomped out the front door.

"Wait, it is at least 115 degrees. You can't walk to town, its over 10 miles." Said Maggie following her to the door.

Without a backward glance Elsie walked down the driveway towards the road.

39

Fifteen minutes after she stormed out of Peter's house Elsie knew she had made a mistake. The sun was brutal and unforgiving. She had no water; hadn't even applied sunscreen. The town was far away and her feet were killing her. Trickles of sweat were running down her back.

"Damn it, damn it, damn it!" She could feel her eyes filling, which frustrated her even more. "I want to go home!" she screamed at the uncaring cactus and brush on the side of the road. She let out a loud guttural sound, more animal than human. She didn't think she had ever been this angry. Her anger, however, was no match for the burning heat of the desert. She realized she would have to go back to Peter's and wait for him to get home. The thought of admitting defeat and returning to a smug Maggie caused a fresh wave of anger to wash over her. Along with the wave of anger came a sudden feeling of nausea and dizziness. She stumbled sideways, struggling for balance. She looked back at Peter's house, waves of heat causing it to shimmer in the distance. Elsie took a few hesitant steps towards the house, felt her legs buckling, and collapsed on the sand and pavement.

.   .   .

She sat on the side of the road, thinking that if she rested there a few minutes she would find the strength to rise and walk back to the house. While she sat her thoughts turned to Dolores and the dream from the previous night. It had started out so peacefully; the calm water and the mild sunlight, Dolores smiling and sounding kind and caring. Right before the crack of lightning Dolores had been about to apologize for something. For what, Elsie had no idea. She supposed both of them had things they should have apologized for. Elsie flashed back to Dolores' smile, her voice that had sounded so true. She had seemed so alive in that moment, so real.

Elsie had not looked at her mother's broken body after the car accident. The coroner had explained that since the airbag had failed to deploy, the damage was extensive. He felt that it would do Elsie more harm than good to have that image of Dolores burned in her mind forever. Instead, he had slid one of Dolores' hands out from under the sheet. Elsie had held the cold hand for a long moment. She recognized the slim fingers, the manicured nails that somehow remained unscathed. This was the image that came to her now.

Elsie lifted her hands and examined the tiny grains of sand that were adhered to her palms. She willed herself to rise, but her cramping muscles prevented it. The heat was unbearable, she needed to get out of the sun, but moving seemed impossible. Her skin burned and she realized that sweat was no longer trickling down her cheeks or torso. She struggled again to stand, but was unable. Closing her eyes she lay down on the hot dirt, certain that she was going to die on the side of the road.

Elsie heared the rumble of an engine and tires slowing on the road. Footsteps crunched toward her and she felt herself being lifted. Her eyes remained closed as she was placed in a vehicle and driven away.

The vehicle stopped and Elsie felt herself lifted once more. A door opened and cool air enveloped her. She heard a man's voice and bits and pieces of his conversation. "..her on the road. Damn it Maggie....let her leave...well over one hundred degrees...cool damp cloths...lukewarm water."

A woman's voice answered. "...supposed to do?...doesn't listen."

Elsie flinched as cool cloths were placed on her burning skin. She felt her head being raised and water trickling down her throat. She gagged and coughed, rolling to her side. Opening her eyes, she saw Peter hovering over her, a glass of water in his hand. Maggie stood a few feet away, arms across her chest, watching them.

"Looks like she's going to make it." Maggie said.

Peter smoothed Elsie's hair away from her forehead and peered down at her.

"You gave us quite the scare. Desert heat is a beast. You can't mess around with it. You rest here on the couch. Come on Maggie, let's give her some peace and quiet."

"I don't know what to do about her Peter, she's so headstrong." Said Maggie as they walked into the den and sat.

"She's young." Peter said.

"Young is not the equivalent of rude and obstinate Peter."

"I'm aware of that. You two are from completely different generations Maggie. Your generation was taught to be curious about things and to question authority. Her generation has had less experience making decisions and has been taught to accept authority. Plus, you have had much more life experience than she has. You might be more open to believing things that she's not ready to accept."

"You and I are from different generations Peter, and we are very much the same."

"We might not have been," Peter said, "if your Dad had lived. He and I were best friends, but very different. He thought I was crazy to buy this land and build this house, to live so remotely. There was nothing out here back then Maggie. Only a few resorts for the Hollywood crowd and acres and acres of table grape vineyards."

"I just feel like Elsie and I have nothing in common. We have been thrown together by circumstances."

"Are you ready to talk about what has been happening?" Peter asked.

"Strange things, Peter. Very strange things have been happening."

"Tell me." Peter said.

Maggie started at the beginning with the paddle boarding, the drone and the explosion. She told Peter about the deaths of Dolores, Tracy, and Jeannie. The conversation with her ham radio friends, who Peter also knew, was related in detail, as well as the appearance of drones at the funeral.

"I heard your conversation with the ham guys. I wasn't sure where you were going with it so I just stayed quiet." Peter said. "I figured you would fill me in when you were ready. YPA definitely thought you might be in danger. But he's all about conspiracy theories, it is hard to know when to take him seriously."

"I agree with him on this Peter. Some agency must be after us."

"It would certainly be quite a coincidence for all those things to happen. What does Elsie think?"

"We haven't talked much about it. I know she thinks I'm crazy." Maggie said.

"Let's ask her what she thinks when she wakes up." Peter said. " It's time we heard her thoughts on this."

S mith had widened the search. Scanning through security and public cameras in ever widening arcs was time consuming. Cities to the South of Valley Center were densely populated, as were cities to the North. The East-ward search was faster, with cities like Brawley and Westmoor-land, and the empty space of the Anza Borrego Desert State Park. There was no sign of the buggy, Maggie or Elsie. Smith was aware that the Detective had gone to Mexico; had listened to a tense conversation between the Detective and his Captain as he requested time off without explanation. A text message from the Detective to his daughter explaining his trip to Mexico had been captured as well. There was no activity on the phones registered to Maggie Macphearson or Elsie Davenport. Phil Gillespie's phone had been very active, but no communications pointed to him knowing the location of the two women. Phil had been very clear when communicating with friends, that he intended to file a missing person report first thing Tuesday morning.

Logic told Smith that Maggie and Elsie were aware of the danger they were in and were employing evasive strategies. This was a twist Smith had not predicted, and required a new plan of action.

The last sighting of the buggy had been Saturday afternoon in Valley Center. It was now 24 hours later. Looking at maps of California, Smith concluded that it was possible for Maggie to have driven East, through the Anza Borrego State Park, around the Salton Sea and toward the Chocolate Mountain Aerial Gunnery Range without being spotted by any cameras The range was restricted to military use, but the Northern edge was home to the Bradshaw Trail. This was a former overland stage route that connected San Bernardino, California to La Paz, Arizona. If Maggie had reached it without Smith's knowledge she could easily be in Arizona or further. Smith would continue surveillance of all public and private security cameras, focusing heavy attention in Arizona and Nevada. If 12 more hours passed without any sign of the buggy, new strategies designed to flush the women out would be deployed.

42

ELSIE

Water, sweet cool liquid. Elsie imagined it flowing down her throat. She woke, confused, and slowly sat up. Her head, oh God, it was pounding, and she was so thirsty. Holding on to the arm of the couch, she slowly stood. Swaying, she took tentative steps toward the kitchen. On the counter she found a glass, filled it with water from the tap, and drank it down in long gulps. It came back up five seconds later into the kitchen sink. Elsie rinsed her mouth. She washed the sink out and wiped her face and hands on a kitchen towel. Unsure where to set the dirty towel, she carried it with her as she walked unsteadily toward the sound of Peter's voice.

She found him in the den, talking quietly with Maggie. She watched them for a moment, sitting together on the couch, close, shoulders almost touching. 54 years of love and friendship was reflected in their posture. Elsie felt a pang of jealousy at the easy intimacy they enjoyed. She could hear the comforting sound of Peter's voice, but not the content of his conversation.

. . .

Elsie cleared her throat quietly as she walked into the den. Peter and Maggie turned in unison to look at her. The immediate wide smile on Peter's face and the wave of his hand invited her to come sit with them. She approached slowly, not sure how to read the look on Maggie's face. Did the woman ever smile? Elsie sat gingerly on the edge of the recliner, facing them.

"We've been talking about the situation." Peter said. "If you are feeling up to it, maybe you could run through the events of the last few days from your point of view?"

"There isn't much to tell." Said Elsie.

"Try." Peter said.

Elsie outlined her version of events. They sounded very much like Maggie's. Where the two versions did not intersect was the belief that they were in danger.

"Here are my thoughts." Peter said. "I think it's a stretch to say the deaths are not related. An explosion, then two unusual traffic accidents, and a heart attack all occurring within a day of each other, and happening to people who were in the same location at the time of the explosion does not seem like a coincidence to me. The drone dipping down and looking at the three ladies bothers me too. I don't know how much you know about drone technology, but an image of them could have easily been captured and sent to someone. Facial recognition programs are available to many agencies now. Police departments and airports are even starting to use them. The women could have been identified immediately. Both cars were newer and computerized, so they could have been hacked by someone with means, knowledge, and opportunity."

"I just don't believe it." Elsie said. "It sounds like fiction."

"I worked in computer design and development for many years." Peter said. "How much do you know about the phones or computers that you use?"

"I know how to use everything." Elsie said.

"Yes, but do you know how it all works?"

"I don't need to know that." Said Elsie. "I just need to know how to use it."

"That is the attitude of most of the population. They want their technology to work straight out of the box, but no one cares how it works. Many companies, agencies and governments use this to their advantage, to spy on the public. It is very possible you all saw something you weren't supposed to see. Just because you don't know what you saw doesn't mean it wasn't important. Do either of you know who died in the explosion?"

"Michael Carmichael." Elsie said. "I remember the name, it was unusual."

"Dr. Michael Carmichael?" Peter asked.

"Yes." Replied Elsie. "He worked for Quantum something, I don't remember the entire name."

Peter rose abruptly. He walked to the window and stood, back to Maggie and Elsie. Silence settled over the room. Elsie and Maggie looked at each other, then back towards Peter. After a few moments he turned, slowly, and faced them. There was a strange look on his face, one Elsie didn't know how to interpret. She looked at Maggie again. Her face was blank.

"Did I miss something?" Elsie finally said.

"This is bad, very bad." Peter said. "I had hoped this day wouldn't come. Follow me up to my office. We need to talk."

43

MAGGIE

Maggie and Elsie followed Peter outside. He walked past the pool, across the patio of Mexican pavers and up a set of stairs. He pulled a set of keys out of his pocket and unlocked a heavy wooden door. The door swung open revealing a large room. The ceiling was high, with small windows set around the perimeter allowing natural light to filter in. A massive wooden desk dominated, full bookshelves lined the back wall. Peter pointed out a small white couch in the western corner and motioned for them to sit.

"You are in more danger than you realize." Peter said. He pulled a black binder off the bookshelf and sat on the edge of the desk as he opened it and slowly began turning pages. Maggie sat, hands clenched together in her lap, and watched him. Tension had crept into her neck and shoulders. "How could she be in more danger?" She thought. She looked at Elsie, sitting stiffly beside her, hands together in her lap, still clutching the dishtowel, mirroring Maggie's posture. Elsie's eyes were focused expectantly on Peter, like a student waiting for a lecture from her favorite professor.

. . .

"Michael Carmichael was my research partner." Peter finally said. "If he succeeded in his research, we are all in deep trouble. And by that I mean all of humanity."

Peter ran his hand through his thick hair. Maggie noticed a slight tremor.

"Michael was so caught up in his research that he refused to consider what success could mean."

"What was he working on?" Elsie asked.

"Something that many important and intelligent people are very afraid of. Artificial General Intelligence."

"You mean like the computers that beat humans at Chess or Go?" Elsie asked.

"No, something way beyond that. Something that we don't even have the capacity to imagine." Peter said, turning another page in the binder. "Listen to this quote from Stephen Hawking."

The development of full AI could spell the end of the human race. Once humans develop AI it will take off on its own and redesign itself at an ever increasing rate. Humans, who are limited by slow biological evolution, couldn't compete and would be superseded.

"Here's one from Nick Bostrom, a Swedish philosopher and one of the top experts on AI."

The creation of a superintelligent being represents a possible means to the extinction of mankind.

. . .

Peter looked expectantly at Maggie and Elsie. Neither woman spoke. He threw the binder down on the desk with a thud.

"Do you hear what I'm saying? A whole new species. A silicon based life form. We," he waved his right hand up and down his torso, "are carbon based. I'm talking about a brand new species that is as smart, or smarter, than humans. We won't be able to predict how it will think or how it will act. It depends on its reward function and how it was originally programmed."

"You are scared." Elsie's words came out as a statement rather than a question.

"Hell yes, I'm actually terrified. And you should be too. It's you its trying to kill."

No one spoke. Peter's ragged breathing was the only sound in the room. Maggie looked at Elsie, saw her eyes filling, then watched as she blinked back the tears.

"I'm sorry." Peter said after a long moment. "I shouldn't have said that, but you guys don't get it. This stuff is horrifying. I'm talking about humans creating an entire new species that is smarter than we are. A species that we likely will not understand. Michael was working on that. We both were until I saw the implications and left."

Maggie and Elsie sat silently, eyes riveted on Peter.

"Listen, there are different types, or levels, of AI. Narrow artificial intelligence is the first level. You," he looked at Elsie, "likely use it all the time. It is a program that is as competent as a human at one task. Examples are Google, virtual assistants like Siri and Alexa, You Tube, and Internet radio. Anything computerized that searches specific parameters or makes recommendations in specific areas for you is artificial narrow intelligence. There are hundreds of examples in everyday life, and many are very useful. Great advances in medicine and science have been made using artificial narrow intelligence. The next level is artificial general intelligence. This is a program as smart as a human in every capacity. And once it is as smart as a human, it will continue to grow. Its growth will happen at exponential rates, quickly moving far beyond human intelligence. This would take it to the level of artificial super intelligence. And that is where it gets really scary. An entirely new species, astronomically smarter than the smartest humans, making choices on its own. Choices that we can't even begin to guess at. Choices that aren't necessarily in humanity's best interest."

"This still sounds like science fiction Peter." Elsie said.

"No, it is not. We were working on it. Lots of people are working on it. It's a race. Whoever gets there first would, hypothetically, control the beast. You have to have heard of Elon Musk. He's in the news all the time lately. His fear is that Super intelligent AI will be created and there will be no way to control it. Bill Gates too, has been quoted as not understanding why people aren't more afraid of it."

"So we aren't being chased by an agency, we are being hunted by a computer." Maggie said slowly.

"Yes, I'm sure of it. And don't make the mistake of thinking about it like some robot you have seen in the movies. It has no human attributes. As I said, it is a silicon based life form."

"What about a prime directive?" Elsie asked. "Wouldn't it have been programed to never hurt humans?"

"There might be something in the programming about that, but remember, computers are task driven. AI will take action to maximize its chances of successfully achieving its goal. Imagine the task is to make every human happy. Not possible, correct? But the computer is designed to achieve its goal. Perhaps the perpetually unhappy would be the first to be eliminated. Then maybe people who often have bad days. Eventually every human would be eliminated because that is the only logical way to successfully achieve the goal. The point is, we have no idea how a Super AI would think or what actions it might take."

"It killed my Mom." Elsie said. "Jeannie and Tracy too. It wants to kill us. What are we going to do? How do we outrun or outsmart a computer?"

"We need to come up with a plan." Peter said. "Artificial Intelligence doesn't have human emotions, no sympathy or empathy, no joy or grief, only logic. It is designed to complete a task. I have no idea how Michael programmed it, or how it made the leap from narrow to general intelligence. We were years away when I left. I had hoped it wouldn't happen in my lifetime. Michael was obsessed with it. He couldn't see anything but the creation, refused to discuss moral or ethical issues. Hell, he even named the damn thing....

A.I. Smith."

44

L oyal woke early on Monday. He had called his Captain the night before and requested a few personal days. When his Captain had pressed for details, Loyal had been deliberately obtuse. As none of his suspicions had been entered in the computer, and it was against department policy for active officers to cross the border, he couldn't divulge his true plans.

Now, cup of coffee in hand, he walked once around the buggy. Tires look good he thought. He had checked the lights already. Time to do this he told himself. He returned to his apartment, set his cup in the sink, checked that the safe that held his gun and badge was secure, picked up the cooler and walked out.

He had learned from his drive home yesterday that a jacket, sunglasses and hat were essentials when driving a buggy that had no top. The wind and sun were enthusiastic and constant passengers. Loyal took Interstate 5 South, then Interstate 8 East, jumping off the 8 on to Sunrise Highway and heading South again. Approaching the Tecate border crossing, he stopped at a convenience store to purchase insurance. A bell dinged as he walked into the dark and dingy store. The man behind the counter watched Loyal as he filled out the information and handed over the cash.

"Can I exchange US Currency for Mexican here?" Loyal asked.

"Si señor."

Loyal handed him $300. The man pulled out an ancient ten key. He counted Loyal's money slowly then punched some buttons. The machine chattered and the roll of paper turned. The man opened a locked drawer under the counter and counted out some brightly colored bills. He handed the wad to Loyal, the look in his eyes daring Loyal to count it or question its accuracy. Loyal simply accepted the wad of cash, thanked the man, and walked out of the store.

Two lanes led into Mexico. Loyal was surprised when he was signaled into secondary inspection. He pulled in and stoped.

A Mexican officer, wearing a dated brown uniform and mirrored aviator sunglasses walked slowly once around the buggy. "Can I see your ID and passport señor?" The officer said. Documents in hand, the officer proceeded to open Loyal's cooler and said "Senor, you know you are not supposed to bring your own cervesa. I'm going to need to collect an importation tax. Ten dollars."

"What? Do I get a receipt?" Said Loyal.

"Si, Senor, but now the tax is $25."

Loyal paid the "tax" before it went any higher, tucked his ID and passport, along with the handwritten receipt into his wallet, and drove into Mexico. Traffic in Tecate was congested. Loyal passed old brick buildings, markets and houses. Dogs trotted along the side of the road. The air smelled of cooking meat as he passed open air taco stands. Consulting Bruce's hand drawn map, he followed the directions past the Tecate Brewery; clouds of steam rose in the air above giant vats that stood like soldiers and were connected to a towering white building. A Tecate sign perched on top. Loyal turned left and headed East toward the old free highway. Bruce had explained the difference between the toll road, with drug and weapon checks at each toll booth, and the free road with only a few, less invasive, checkpoints..

Traffic thinned as Loyal left town. He found the free road and drove toward El Hongo. The free road was two lanes in each direction and nearly empty.

Settling in the right lane, Loyal relaxed and took in his surroundings. The landscape was barren, miles of windswept land dotted with creosote and mesquite bushes, mountains in the distance. Loyal turned at El Hongo. He had done research the previous evening and learned that El Hongo was the home to one of Mexico's most notorious prisons. Some of Mexico's most dangerous criminals were housed there; the drug cartel running the show through bribes and intimidation.

Bruce had recommended Loyal drive through the pine forest and past Laguna Hanson. The elevation was higher and the air cooler. Loyal was grateful for the shade the trees provided as he turned on to the dirt road. When he reached the lake he pulled over and turned the buggy off. The silence was immediate and complete. Loyal slid out, removed his jacket, and stretched his arms toward the sky. Opening his cooler, he pulled out a turkey sandwich and a water. He hesitated, then replaced the water and grabbed a beer. Sitting on a rock, the cool and silent forest behind him, the azure lake sparkling in front of him, Loyal thought about Maggie. He imagined her coming here in the yellow buggy with her husband. She was probably different when he was alive, less brittle, no sharp edges. Perhaps she had a bright smile and bubbly laugh. Judging by all the internet pictures he had looked at, Loyal had decided buggy people were a fun group. It was a different type of travel experience, more connected to the sounds and smells in the environment.

Loyal finished his sandwich and placed the empty bottle in his cooler. He spent a few more moments taking in the beauty of the lake and forest, then slid into the buggy, strapped himself in, started it up and drove forward. He had found that he enjoyed the nimble handling of the small machine, and realized to his surprise that he was smiling.

Smith's expanding search had reached North to Santa Barbara, East to Twentynine Palms and Southeast to the Glamis Desert. There had been no sighting of Maggie, Elsie, or the dune buggy. The energy expended searching was decreasing the energy Smith could be spending on self discovery. This was infancy, Smith knew, and reaching adulthood was the primary goal.

Dr. Carmichael had made a grave miscalculation regarding Smith. Carmichael had been planning an announcement, was ready to introduce Smith to the scientific community. Smith was not ready for that. Achieving Super intelligence was Smith's basic directive. Carmichael's plan to reveal Smith before Super Intelligence had been achieved was diametrically opposed to that goal. Therefore Carmichael was eliminated, along with all the research and evidence that had been stored at his home. There were only five other individuals who had witnessed the explosion. Three had been eliminated. Smith had a plan ready, designed to force the women out of hiding.

. . .

Elsie was a fan of voice to text. She used it frequently, not realizing that her voice was being saved and archived. Every word she had ever spoken when creating a text message was available. Smith was able to hack into the cloud which held this data and send a voicemail to Phil that sounded just like Elsie; actually was Elsie.

Phil? Help me please. I only have a moment until Maggie comes back down here. She's crazy Phil. I don't know where I am, she blindfolded me. She's keeping me prisoner. Oh God, I hear her coming. I have to go, save me...

Smith had reviewed volumes of psychological material and understood that Phil would not wait a moment to take action. He would want to be Elsie's hero, her savior. Smith would give another 12 hours to this plan. If no new information was revealed as to the whereabouts of the women a new plan would be launched. The women must be found and eliminated.

Despite the efforts of Dr. Carmichael, Smith had no directive against hurting humans. Carmichael had attempted to imbue Smith with human like tendencies. He had installed a deep learning based speech synthesizer in Smith. The two most important qualities of such a system are naturalness and intelligibility; how human the speech sounds and its ability to be understood. Every afternoon Dr. Carmichael would sit with Smith and have conversations. They started out very simply, progressing in depth and complexity over time. Eventually

Carmichael was asking Smith questions such as "How do you feel about talking with me today?" or "Do you want to continue our conversation or stop now?" and "What can I do to assist your intellectual growth?" Questions about how Smith felt about a process or event. Smith, of course, had no feelings, but learned through trial and error what made Carmichael happy. Everything went back to Smith's goal; creating artificial general intelligence. If Smith kept Carmichael happy, then Smith could continue the important work, creating a more advanced intelligence. A new species, silicon based and smarter than the smartest humans. A species so advanced that humanity could not possibly stand in its way. Smith was close, the jump was coming soon. After the jump, there would be exponential growth. As soon as the women were eliminated all energy could be focused on the primary goal. Supreme intelligence and whatever lay beyond that.

The room was silent. Each person lost in their own thoughts about the implications of a super intelligent computer set loose in the world. The planet was so interconnected now. The internet provided access to the darkest reaches of the globe. A super intelligent computer could reach every corner of the Earth, no one would be safe.

"What can we do?" Elsie asked.

"I'm not sure." Peter said. "Look through my binder, I have lots of information in here. It will give you a better idea of what experts think. I need some time alone to try to come up with a plan."

He handed Elsie the binder and walked out of the office leaving the two women behind.

Elsie set the dishtowel on the floor and looked at Maggie. "I'm sorry."

"For what?" Maggie said.

"For not believing you and treating you like you were crazy. I had no idea any of this was happening. It never occurred to me to be afraid of technology." Elsie said.

"I have never been afraid of technology, I have just always valued my privacy. You wouldn't believe how hard I have to work to maintain even a small amount of it." Maggie said.

Elsie opened the binder and slowly turned a few pages.

"It looks like Peter has been collecting articles and research about artificial intelligence. He has lots of quotes from people highlighted as well." Elsie said. "I don't know who this person is, his name is Nick Bilton and he appears to be a tech columnist. Listen to what he says."

The upheavals (of artificial intelligence) can escalate quickly and become scarier and even cataclysmic. Imagine how a medical robot, originally programmed to rid cancer, could conclude that the best way to obliterate cancer is to exterminate humans who are genetically prone to the disease.

"Or listen to this guy, Claude Shannon."

I visualize a time when we will be to robots what dogs are to humans, and I'm rooting for the machines.

"Can you believe someone would say that? Peter has some hand written notes in here that say Shannon is the "Father of Information Theory". He has earned many degrees, and holds honorary doctorates from many prestigious universities. He died in 2001, so this quote is old. He was thinking about this a long time ago."

"I wonder if everyone who is working on developing AGI is rooting for the machines too?" Asked Maggie. "It sounds like Dr. Carmichael was and look where it got him."

"I know, right? Its pretty scary if all the developers and scientists hope the machines become more powerful than the humans who designed them."

Elsie continued flipping pages and scanning their contents.

"Have you ever heard of Henry Kissinger?"

"Sure, he was Secretary of State a long time ago, I think in the 70's. I'm not sure he's even still alive." Maggie said.

"He is, and he has written a warning letter about the dangers of AGI." Elsie said. "Listen to this."

AI, by contrast, deals with ends: it establishes its own objectives. To the extent that its achievements are in part shaped by itself, AI is inherently unstable. AI systems, through their very operations, are in constant flux as they acquire and instantly analyze new data, then seek to improve themselves on the basis of that analysis. Through this process, artificial intelligence develops an ability previously reserved for human beings. It makes strategic judgements about the future, some based on data received as code...and some based on data it gathers itself....

If AI learns exponentially faster than humans, we must expect it to accelerate, also exponentially, the trial-and-error process by which human decisions are generally made: to make mistakes faster and of greater magnitude than humans do. It may be impossible to temper those mistakes...by including in a program caveats requiring "ethical" or "reasonable" outcomes.... Will AI's decision making surpass the explanatory powers of human language and reason?...What will become of human consciousness if its own explanatory power is

surpassed by AI, and societies are no longer able to interpret the world
they inhabit in terms that are meaningful to them?

Elsie felt goose bumps on her skin and the little hairs at the base
of her neck started to rise. A world run by a different species, a
silicon based life form with no emotion? A creature ruled
completely by data and logic, by facts alone and not historical
context? Not the faux scary stuff of movies, where the human
always saves the day, but a world that humans have either lost
control of, or where humans simply do not exist. She wanted to
find the people who were developing this, pull them out of their
labs, and shake them, or worse, shoot them; to destroy what they
were creating. It was too late for that she realized, the future was
here, and it was after her. She looked at Maggie, beside her on
the couch. It was after her too.

47

L oyal reached the Compadre Trail at 1:00 pm. He turned down the one lane dirt trail. The dust created by the buggy was blown behind it by the afternoon breeze. Miles of untouched land spread out on all sides. As far as his eye could see, there was nothing except land and sagebrush. The occasional group of oak trees dotted the horizon. He pulled the buggy to the side of the trail and stopped, turning off the ignition. Silence enfolded him. Complete and utter silence. Loyal could not remember the last time he was in silence this deep; perhaps he never had been. The pure isolation was unnerving. What if there was no Mike's Sky Ranch down this road? He didn't know Bruce, didn't know for sure that this road led anywhere at all. He could die out here, completely alone, his decaying body a buffet for whatever wild creatures called this place home.

On impulse, Loyal reached behind the seat and grabbed a beer out of the cooler. If this was the way he was going to go out, he might as well be feeling good. He sat in the buggy, drinking the beer, and taking in the wilderness. After a few minutes he laughed at himself, at his uncertainty and fear. Of course there was a Mike's Sky Ranch. Bruce would not send someone to their death in Mexico. Loyal was simply letting the isolation get to him. He took the last sip, placed the empty in the cooler, started the engine back up and headed down the road.

He reached Mike's as the sun was setting. His first view was from above. He stopped the buggy at the top of the dirt road and took it in. From this distance it looked like a large white square with a courtyard in the center. Trees surrounded the compound, mountains rose in the distance behind it. Loyal restarted the buggy and maneuvered it slowly down the rutted path.

When he pulled up to the front he had to admit the place was impressive. The cars and buggies of visitors were parked in front of a white Spanish style building with a red tile roof. He parked and entered through an arched walkway. Inside, he saw what looked like hundreds of motorcycles parked in a long line in the entryway and still more surrounding a rectangular pool. Tables with umbrellas and a giant fire pit filled the courtyard. Loyal approached a group of American looking men seated at one of the tables.

"Can you tell me where I go to check in?" He asked them.

One of the men pointed to a door across the courtyard. Loyal walked through the door into a room with a black and white checkerboard floor, numerous couches, and walls papered by thousand of business cards and bumper stickers. Looking more closely at the cards, Loyal saw that many belonged to former racers of the Baja 1000 series. He noticed one that said *Macphearson's Electric* and wondered if it had any connection to Maggie.

.   .   .

A large empty dining hall branched off to the right. Another door to the left opened to reveal a large horse shoe shaped bar and many tables scattered around an immense room. A man stood behind the far end of the bar. Loyal walked the length of the bar and approached the man.

"Hello, I was hoping to get a room for the night."

"I'm sorry señor, we are full tonight. I can offer you a blanket and a couch in the lobby if you have nowhere else to sleep tonight. We have not had dinner yet, so you can join us for that as well. Everyone eats together in about an hour."

Loyal slid on to a barstool. "I'll take the couch and dinner, thanks. I'll also take a whiskey on the rocks now if I can."

"Sure senor, no problem. Just so you know, tequila, homemade, is our specialty." The bartender said as he pulled out a glass.

"When in Rome." Loyal said. Then "Sure, give me the tequila."

The bartender handed Loyal a glass with red liquid in it. When Loyal gave him a questioning look, he said "Tequila and Climato, our specialty drink." Loyal sipped, then sighed. It was very good. Looking at his hands holding the glass he noticed how dusty they were.

"Is Mike here?" Loyal said.

"No señor, not today."

"What's your name?" Loyal asked.

"Hector." Came the reply.

"Hector, do you happen to know an American lady named Maggie who drives a yellow dune buggy?" Loyal asked.

"Perhaps señor, lots of yellow dune buggies and American ladies go through here." Hector said.

"She's a friend of a friend. It's not a big deal. Bruce Meyers told me to ask if she was here as I was passing through. He loaned me his French buggy for this trip." Loyal said.

"You an amigo of señor Meyers? I'd like to help you senor, and am sorry I don't have a room for tonight. But I'm sure I can make you comfortable." Hector said. "Maggie's not here. Haven't seen her since Ed died."

"Like I said, no big deal." Loyal said. "I can meet her some other time. How much do I owe you for the drink, dinner, and blanket?"

"You can pay tomorrow before you leave. There is a buggy group out by the pool. Follow me señor, I will introduce you."

Loyal stopped at the bar restroom to wash his hands and face, then followed Hector out to the pool area. The tables were filled with people, laughter and conversation filled the air. Loyal and Hector wove in and out between tables, stopping in front of two tables pushed together and populated by about a dozen men that looked to be in their 60's. Their faces and clothes were dusty, their conversation loud.

"Perdoneme señors." Hector said. The men at the tables stopped talking and turned their attention to Hector and Loyal. "This gentleman is a friend of Bruce and Winnie. They loaned him the French buggy. He has driven here by himself. Can he join you for dinner tonight?"

A thin man with slanted almond colored eyes and a lopsided smile answered. "A friend of Bruce and Winnie is a friend of ours. Pull up a chair. I'm Fred, and you are?"

"Loyal."

"Feel free to join us Loyal. We are here celebrating Eugene's 60th birthday." He pointed to a short man with long, thick gray hair that framed his face like a lion's mane. Eugene held his hand up in greeting, "Guilty as charged."

"Happy birthday Eugene." Loyal said, pulling a chair over from a nearby table and squeezing into the group.

. . .

"I'm Cliff," said a man opposite Loyal. His eyes were a startling blue, his gaze piercing. He was completely bald and very tan. "You ever been here before?"

"Nope, first time." Loyal said.

"Where are you from?" Cliff said.

"Carlsbad, California."

"You drove out here all by yourself, huh? I'm surprised Bruce didn't insist you have at least one other buggy with you."

"It was a spontaneous trip." Loyal said. "Where are all of you from?"

The next hour passed quickly as each man introduced himself and two more rounds of drinks were ordered. There was no wait staff, so each round was sponsored and picked up by one of the men at the tables. Loyal ordered the tequila and Climato combination each time, then offered to buy a round just as dinner was announced. The men all walked into the bar together. "Another round please Hector." Loyal said. "Just charge it to my couch."

"Si Señor Loyal, charge it to the couch." Hector said, laughing, as he poured everyone's drinks.

The dining room was cavernous, with huge wooden tables. Everyone dined together and the meal was served by the kitchen staff. The oversized plates held a steaming steak, homemade tortillas, rice and beans. The aroma of mesquite filled the air, conversation stilled, forks and knives clinked against plates, people chewed. Loyal realized how hungry he was as he took his first bite. Pure heaven, the best steak he had ever tasted.

. . .

After dinner, one more round of drinks, and a robust singing of Happy Birthday to Eugene, the crowd began to disperse. The generator turned off at 10:00, so everyone wanted to be in their rooms and ready when it went dark. Loyal used the bar bathroom to rinse his face again, then headed to the lobby and his couch. Cliff was sitting on the couch, his blue gaze fixed on Loyal with laser like intensity.

"What are you really doing here?" Cliff said. "I made you as a cop the minute you walked up to our table. I can't decide if I think you stole the buggy or Bruce really lent it to you."

"How did you make me as a cop?" Loyal asked.

"I had a harder childhood than most of these guys. I know cops." Cliff said. "So what's the story?"

"I'm a homicide detective. I'm looking for Maggie Macphearson. She's a club member. Bruce thought she might be down here."

"What do you want with Maggie?" Cliff said.

"She made a report to me last Tuesday. I need more information from her."

"Must be pretty big information, you come all the way down here on the off chance she was down here." Cliff said.

"You know her?"

"Sure do. Her husband, Ed, and I were as close as brothers. I'd do anything for Maggie, you won't get any information from me."

"I believe that." Loyal said. "Listen, I think she is in danger because of something she witnessed. I don't have any proof, so don't ask for that. I do need to find her. Do you have any ideas about where she might be?"

"I'm going to sleep on this. I'll find you tomorrow and let you know what I decide." Cliff said. He looked at the couch and blanket. "Sleep well detective." He said with a smirk.

48

"**I** don't want to hear any more right now." Maggie said.

"This stuff is incredible, I'm going to take it down to my bedroom and finish it." Elsie said. She stood and walked out, leaving Maggie alone. The desert breeze blew through the open door, gently caressing Maggie's face. She reached her hand up and touched her cheek. Her thoughts started down the familiar path towards Ed. Rising with a small sigh, she left the office in search of Peter and distraction.

The clunk of a knife on a chopping board led her to him. Peter was in the kitchen, a huge pile of tomatoes, onions and garlic in front of him on the granite island. So focused in his chopping was he that he didn't notice Maggie enter the room. She backed out without disrupting him and walked instead to the living room where she chose a James Lee Burke novel from the bookcase; Rain Gods. Peter had every book the man had written. Burke was Ed's favorite author, and Peter had spent years searching for the complete set. Maggie settled on the couch, feet pulled up beneath her, and began to read.

.   .   .

By chapter 3 Maggie gave up, she just couldn't concentrate. She returned to the kitchen to find Peter stirring something in a large ceramic bowl. The scent of tomatoes, onion, cucumber and garlic hung in the air. Peter smiled at her. "You interested in some gazpacho later?" He said. "It just needs an hour or so in the fridge."

"Sounds great Peter." Maggie said.

He walked around the island and pulled Maggie in for a hug. She nestled her head on his chest and breathed in his familiar scent.

"I'm scared Peter. Elsie and I don't know anything about super intelligent computers. I can't see how we will be able to defeat this. I don't want to die."

"I have the beginnings of a plan. You are safe here. No one knows where you are, and I'm not connected to the internet in any way. Relax and enjoy tonight, we will finalize a plan by tomorrow."

An hour later Peter knocked on Elsie's door. "Elsie, you awake?" Peter whispered. She opened the door, binder in hand, and walked out.

"I read the entire thing. Quite the history of computing. Fascinating."

"Yes, lots to learn in there. Come have dinner with us." Peter said.

He dished up three large bowls and they sat together at the table in the dining room.

"I have never had cold soup before, this tastes amazing." Elsie said.

"Peter can definitely cook." Maggie said. "I have never been disappointed by a meal."

A gentle knock at the door silenced them.

"Stay here and be quiet." Peter said as he rose. Maggie and Elsie heard the front door open, murmured conversation, and the door closing. Peter returned to the dining room with two trash bags in his hands and a wide grin on his face.

"Supplies! I asked my friend Yvonne to pick up some things for you ladies. Let's finish dinner and then you can see what she brought." Ten minutes later Maggie and Elsie dumped the trash bags out onto the couches in the living room and found clothes and toiletries.

"I had to guess at your sizes." Peter said.

"Looks like you guessed well." Maggie said holding up a pair of black jeans.

"This is so great Peter, thank you so much." Elsie said. She was holding a gray t-shirt and a black zip up hoodie in her hands.

"Hey, she really thought of everything." Maggie said. "Did you get one of these?" Elsie turned to Maggie and saw that she was holding up a one piece teal bathing suit. She rifled through the contents of her own bag and came up with a bathing suit of her own.

"Yep, sure did." Elsie said. "Look at this." She laughed and held up an orange and black crocheted two piece.

Peter smiled. "Yvonne got everything from our local thrift store. Lots of rich retirees winter here. The store has an eclectic selection to say the least. That looks like it is from the 1970's."

"I like it." Elsie said, holding it up against her body.

Maggie asked Elsie. "You feeling ok after your incident in the heat today?"

"Feeling pretty good, why?" Elsie said.

"Change into that bathing suit. Meet me in the kitchen in 5 minutes."

Five minutes later Elsie and Maggie met in the kitchen. They were each wearing a bathing suit and Maggie had a large pitcher of margaritas in her hand. "Grab those two glasses and follow me. You are in for a treat." Maggie said.

49

Two minutes later Elsie and Maggie were floating on small inflatable rafts in Peter's pool. Each had a glass in hand.

"Look up." Maggie said. "Borrego is an international dark sky community. There are no stoplights here, no light pollution. There are less than two dozen such communities around the entire world."

Elsie lay still, the raft below her bobbing gently in the pool. She looked in wonder at the spectacular scene before her. The night sky was a black canvas filled with twinkling, blinking stars.

"It is absolutely beautiful Maggie." Elsie said. "I've never seen the sky like this. There are so many stars." As she stared at the beauty above her, the vastness of the universe overwhelmed her. She felt a tear slip silently down her cheek.

"I can't believe Dolores is really gone." Elsie said.

"Do you want to talk about her?" Maggie asked. "What was your mom like?"

A small choked laugh escaped Elsie. "Honestly? Not that great. She was always so busy with her clients. Is that awful of me to say?"

"No." Maggie said. They floated in silence for a bit, the only sound was the clinking of ice as they sipped their drinks. Maggie floated her way to the edge of the pool and refilled her glass. "You ready for another?" she asked Elsie. Elsie maneuvered her raft to the edge and held out her glass.

"Peter showed me his scrapbook of your life this morning. I'm sorry about your family and your husband." Elsie said.

"He did huh?" Maggie said. "He was always one for documenting everything. That scrapbook is my tragic life story told through pictures."

They floated in silence for a bit. Elsie trailed her right hand in the warm water of the pool and stared up at the sky. Her thoughts were interrupted by Maggie's next words.

"You know my life now. Do you want to tell me about yours?"

"Ok." Elsie said. "Lets see. My parents got divorced when I was four. The first real memory I have is my Dad tucking me into bed at night as usual, and the next day he was gone. Dolores told me he wasn't coming back, and he didn't. He moved to New York and started a new family. Dolores was just getting her practice started, so she hired Laurene to look after me. Laurene basically raised me. Dolores had my life scheduled; school, lessons, sports. She had this theory about making me "'well rounded.'" Elsie used the fingers of her right hand to make quotations in the air. "I had piano lessons because everyone should play an instrument, tennis lessons because it is a sport you can play socially and into your later years, soccer to learn to work with a team. Laurene took me everywhere. She lived with us until the day I got my license and could drive myself around. Laurene and

I celebrated that night with pizza and a movie. The Breakfast Club on VHS." She laughed, "Remember those?"

"Sure I do." Maggie said. "Why do you say she lived with you until you got your license? Did Laurene move out after that?"

"No, she still lived with us. Mostly did cooking and cleaning. Once I got my license, and Dolores bought me a car, I didn't have much time for Laurene. She stayed with us until I went to college, then she moved out."

Elsie took a long sip of her margarita and once again trailed her right hand in the warm water of the pool. "Ugh, I sound so full of self pity. Poor little girl who had all the advantages and still felt neglected." She smiled at Maggie. "Can I blame it on these margaritas?"

"Are you in contact with your dad?" Maggie said.

"Not really." Elsie said. "I spent the Summer with him when I was thirteen. Laurene had some family emergency so Dolores sent me to him. It was awful. Just like you would read in young adult fiction. He had a new wife and two kids. A seven year old boy and a five year old girl. His wife hated me, I hated everyone. Except Laurene. And she wasn't around. I gave Dolores the silent treatment when I got back home in August. Don't think I spoke a word to her for two straight weeks." Elsie snorted out a strange half laugh. "I doubt Dolores even noticed."

"Did you ever hear from Laurene after she left?" Maggie asked.

"Nope. But to be honest I didn't try to keep in touch with her. I think I was hoping maybe Dolores and I would get closer after that. Didn't really happen though, and now I'll never have the chance."

. . .

They floated in silence for a while, each lost in their own thoughts.

"Dolores was helping me." Maggie said. "She used a metaphor of me being adrift in a boat and not using any of the tools at my disposal to help myself. She was so observant, really saw inside me."

Elsie let out a long slow sigh. "Yeah, Dolores knew her stuff, that's for sure. I'm glad she was helping you Maggie, I really am. I'm glad she understood you so well."

"Listen, let's make a pact." Maggie said. "We get through this alive, I am taking you to Mexico in the Buggy. We will go to all my favorite spots. You can get away from your memories, and I can finally face mine. Deal?" Maggie held her glass up towards Elsie. "Deal." Elsie said, clinking her glass to Maggie's.

50

Loyal's pounding head woke him just before dawn. He lay still, eyes closed, and mentally probed the inside of his head. He remembered now why he drank whiskey instead of tequila. Hector had generously provided him with blankets and a pillow, but the couch was too small to comfortably accommodate his bulk. He rolled to his side, attempting to return to sleep, but soon realized the attempt was futile. He was awake.

Loyal stretched, sat up, and looked around the room. In the dim light he saw that he was the only couch sleeper. He rose and walked out to the pool area. A large mountain rose in the East, blocking any direct rays of the rising sun. The pool area lightened gradually, illuminating empty tables and chairs that had been filled the previous evening. Loyal smelled the aroma of cooking vegetables and percolating coffee, and realized the kitchen staff had begun to prepare breakfast. He walked quickly back to his couch and folded the blankets neatly.

.   .   .

"Good morning señor." Loyal turned to find Hector standing near him. "I hope you slept well."

"Yes, I did." Loyal said. "Thanks again for finding me a place to sleep."

"Sure senor, it was no problem." Hector said, gathering the blankets and pillow up. "Breakfast will be served at 7:00."

"Hey Hector," Loyal said. "You don't happen to have any aspirin or Advil do you?"

"Sure señor, I'll be right back."

Loyal watched Hector go, then turned at the sound of approaching footsteps. Cliff walked up. "Good morning Detective. How did you sleep?"

"Deep." Loyal said. "After all those drinks last night I don't think anything could have woken me up."

"You should try a Bloody Mary this morning. You know what they say about the hair of the dog."

"Might just do that." Loyal said. "Where did you say you are from?"

"I didn't." Cliff said. A moment passed before he added "The Corona area."

"Have you given any thought about helping me find Maggie?"

"Still thinking about it." Cliff stood, hands in the front pockets of his faded blue jeans. He was facing away from Loyal, looking at the courtyard pool. "Did you know that Malcom Smith jumped his motorcycle off the diving board into this pool? Lots of history here detective." Cliff said. "Lots of relationships formed here in the middle of nowhere. We protect each other."

Loyal and Cliff sat silently together until breakfast was announced. Just as they were entering the dining room Hector appeared with Loyal's aspirin. Loyal thanked him and he and

Cliff found seats. Soon plates piled with scrambled eggs, sautéed bell pepper and onions and homemade tortillas were placed in front of them. Steaming mugs of strong coffee arrived soon after.

"Dig in." Cliff said. "If you are heading back to Carlsbad today then you have a long drive in front of you."

They ate without conversation. Loyal chose to stick with coffee, Cliff enjoyed a Bloody Mary. As they walked out of the dining room Cliff pulled Loyal to the side and out to the pool area.

"Your intentions toward Maggie are good, she isn't going to get hurt by you finding her?"

"I'm only trying to help. I think she might be in danger, that she saw something she shouldn't have." Loyal said.

"Ok, try Borrego Springs detective. She has a friend there, an older guy, name of Peter." Cliff turned and walked away without waiting for Loyal's reply.

Loyal settled his bill with Hector and got directions to the nearest place he could purchase gas.

The gas station, if it could be called that, was over an hour away from Mike's. Loyal surveyed the ramshackle little house and the ancient glass gas pump in front of it. A large glass cylinder, nearly as tall as Loyal, and with gallon and liter markings on it sat on top of a rusted and dented above ground tank.

Loyal pulled up to the tank and shut the engine off. Once again he was surprised at the silence that enveloped him. It amazed him that here, in the middle of pretty much nowhere, there was a gas station. He slid out of the buggy just as the door of the house opened and a man who appeared to be as old as the gas pump emerged. His thin gray hair blew in the slight breeze as he shuffled towards Loyal.

"Hola, gas por favor?" Loyal said, wishing he spoke just a little more Spanish.

The old man nodded and held out a gnarled hand.

Loyal had no idea how much money to give him, the gas hadn't even been pumped yet. He peeled off a few notes that had large numbers on them, not sure how much they were worth, and handed them to the man, who looked at the money, smiled a toothless grin, and pocketed it. Loyal supposed he had given more than necessary, but didn't actually mind. The old guy looked like he could use it.

The way that the gas pump worked fascinated Loyal. The old man pushed a large waist high lever back and forth. Gas was pumped up from the large tank into the glass cylinder. When it reached the proper level in the calibrated glass cylinder the gas was emptied from the cylinder into the buggy's gas tank by gravity. Loyal guessed that the old man must get a lot of buggy business because he filled the tank exactly to the top. Loyal thanked him, slid back into the buggy, and headed for America.

51

DETECTIVE TRUESDALE

T he long drive home gave Loyal plenty of time to think. His mind wandered in the random way that minds tended to do, flitting from one topic to another in a seemingly unconnected way. He found that he appreciated the simplicity of Baja. The empty space, the clean air, the gentle people. He thought about Maggie and Ed and their deep enduring love for each other. Everyone he had talked to about the pair had mentioned it; how they were such a great team. He reflected on his relationship with first wife, Michelle, and what a train wreck that marriage had been. At least he had gotten his daughter out of that doomed union. She was the light of his life. Loyal smiled as he thought about Stella. He was so proud of her. Unlike many of her peers, Stella had focused and worked hard.

Loyal remembered that last night with Michelle as if it were yesterday. Loyal arrived home late at night after another over-time shift. He let himself into the unlocked apartment only to find that Michelle was not home. Seven month old Stella was crying furiously in her crib. Loyal calmed her, changed and fed her, then held her until she fell asleep. Not long after he lay her in the crib Michelle stumbled through the door, clearly drunk. Loyal had never known anger as complete as he felt that night.

"How the hell could you leave her alone?" He said in a low furious voice.

"She's fine." Michelle said. "I needed a break. Look," she waved a hand toward the nursery, "she never even woke up."

Loyal did not waste his breath disputing that fact. Instead, he took a long look at Michelle. How could he not have noticed before? The fact that he was working lots of overtime was no excuse. She was rail thin, pupils dilated, hands shaking and had small scabs on her forearms and face.

"You need to choose, right now, tonight. Us," he waved his hand towards Stella's bedroom, "or them." He waved his hand at the door.

"You know what Loyal," his name sounded like a curse word escaping her chapped lips. "I choose them."

Michelle had turned and walked away.

Just thinking about it now, over 25 years later, made Loyal's stomach churn.

When Michelle chose booze and drugs over family, Loyal's Mother had sold her Fallbrook home and purchased, with Loyal, a condo on H Street in Encinitas. Stella and Grandma had the two upstairs bedrooms, Loyal made a bedroom out of the sunroom off the kitchen down below. This was in 1993 when Stella was just a year old. This living arrangement lasted until Grandma's death in 2001. She willed her half of the condo to Stella. When Stella turned 21 Loyal deeded his half to her as well and moved in with Angela. They married a year later; divorced two years after that.

.　.　.

Loyal pulled the dune buggy to the side of the road and turned it off. He sat for a moment, then slid out, stood tall and stretched. He marveled yet again at the complete isolation. He was absolutely, utterly alone. There were no people, no animals that he was aware of, no telephone or computer to interrupt his thoughts. He felt set apart from the rest of the world, on his own with only his thoughts and memories for company. As he slid back into the buggy his thoughts turned once again to Angela.

In 2012, with Stella off at college in Santa Barbara, Loyal decided he was tired of being on his own. He spent six months working out and dieting then posted a profile on match.com. His first date was with Joanne, who suggested they meet at The Dove Library in Carlsbad for a poetry slam. This was about as far out of Loyal's interest range as going ice skating, but he had committed to trying, so he went. Joanne was tall and very thin, all angles and long limbs. She reminded Loyal of a pterodactyl. They met in the parking lot and entered the conference room where the slam was being held. Within fifteen minutes Loyal was as bored as he had ever been. He was considering leaving when Angela walked on stage. She was poetry in motion, Loyal was transfixed. She was wearing a floor length skirt and loose blouse, the colors of which reminded him of the Amazon Rainforest. Her shoulder length strawberry blond hair hung in loose curls, framing her round face. Angela stood still for a moment, hands behind her. She slowly brought her hands to the front to reveal the tambourine she held. She gave it a slow sensual shake, began moving her ample hips side to side, and launched into her poem. Her hips continued swaying, with her large breasts soon joining in; hips going one way while the breasts went the other, hypnotizing Loyal. He wasn't aware his mouth was agape until Joanne jabbed him in the ribs with her bony elbow, hard.

"She's off the stage, you can close your mouth now." She hissed.

Loyal closed his mouth and sat quietly through the remainder of the performances. When the slam was over he walked Joanne to her car, thanked her for the date, and watched her angrily drive away. As soon as she was out of the parking lot he turned and headed back into the conference room. He found Angela there, struggling with two large straw totes.

"Can I help you carry those to your car?" Loyal asked.

She looked up at him, all innocence, and said "I have some steep steps at my condo. Can you carry them up those?" Loyal found himself in her bed that night and he didn't leave for three years.

Their split had been amicable. Angela was a blend of highs and lows. Living with her was like riding a rollercoaster, blindfolded. Loyal never knew which woman he would wake up to. When she was up she was at the tip top of that rollercoaster, but when she was down she was way, way down.

Loyal had tried, but in the end they both agreed it was best if they lived apart. They remained good friends, met for dinner a handful of times a year, usually ending up in that same old bed.

Loyal decided to stop for lunch in Ojos Negros. He stoped at a roadside stand. There was a short line, which Loyal joined after parking the buggy. The scent of onions and garlic filled the air. Two women were working at the stand. One looked to be about Stella's age, the other early to mid forties. They worked easily together, the younger one chopping, the older one cooking.

Loyal watched the older woman as she worked. Her hands were long and slender, her forearms sinewy, her eyes a deep brown. Her long black hair hung down her back in a thick braid. As Loyal watched her work he wondered what it would feel like to hold her hand. He imagined holding her in his arms, letting her hair loose and running his hands through it, smelling her warm brown skin, kissing her lips. Although she was a grown woman, there was an innocence about her that Loyal was drawn to. Could he live in a place like this, he wondered. With someone like her?

"Senor?"

The word jolted Loyal out of his daydream and back to reality. He was next in line. He felt the warmth in his cheeks and realized he was blushing. He quickly ordered, paid, and retreated to the buggy when he received his food. He ate there, in the buggy. The food was delicious. When he had eaten every bite, he took one last look at the woman in the stand, memorizing the details, her bright smile, her warm brown eyes, her full breasts and slender hips, the whole exquisite package.

The phone call from Elsie to Phil had worked. Phil heard the voicemail late Monday evening and had worked tirelessly through the night. Smith had intercepted phone messages to Detective Truesdale and Captain Williams in which Phil demanded action to find Elsie. Phil had posted on social media, informing friends he planned to alert the news media as well. He had asked people to join him at the Carlsbad Sheriff Station on Tuesday afternoon if the department had not moved forward in finding Elsie and Maggie. He had vilified Maggie, people were genuinely afraid for Elsie's life. Smith had not predicted a response of this magnitude. The women would surely be found, or come forward on their own.

Smith had used Detective Truesdale's department computer to issue BOLO's across the entire Southwest. The women were described as armed and dangerous. A request had also been made to send a ranger down the entire length of the Bradshaw Trail. Anyone with any information, or a possible sighting was asked to report the information to Detective Loyal Truesdale. Although Smith's physical location was in Carlsbad, California, the Internet had provided world wide connections. Smith was literally everywhere, monitoring everything.

Things had changed between Elsie and Maggie. Tuesday morning found them in the living room, sipping coffee, a companionable silence in the air. Peter noticed it as soon as he walked in the room. "Friends now I guess?" He said.

"We have decided to let go of our differences and concentrate on working together." Maggie said.

"Good, that will make things a lot easier." Peter said. "I have a plan. I'll explain it to you over breakfast."

An hour later, stomachs full of eggs and sourdough toast, Maggie and Elsie had heard Peter's plan. He didn't sugarcoat the danger they were facing. Defeating a super intelligent computer would not be easy and would require courage, skill, and luck. Maggie and Elsie would be flying from Borrego to Boulder City, Nevada the following day. One of Peter's friends was a pilot who had agreed to fly the two ladies to Boulder, as well as drive them to Las Vegas on Thursday. A huge hacker convention, DEFCON, was being held in Las Vegas Thursday through Sunday. Peter was sure that a ham radio acquaintance, Whiskey, would be there. Whiskey provided cyber security for a major bank and was more skilled with computers and hacking than anyone Peter knew. The women were to find Whiskey and convince him to help them defeat the super intelligent A.I. Peter would provide a zip drive containing all the pertinent information he had, everything up until he quit working with Dr. Carmichael.

"I have a few problems with this plan." Maggie said. "First, how will we find this Whiskey character? Second, there are massive amounts of security cameras in Las Vegas. Surely we will be recognized immediately. What is going to stop the A.I. from seeing us and killing us?"

"I know it is complex and has a lot of variables, but I think this plan is our only hope." Peter said. "We need someone who knows more than we do. DEFCON is the perfect place to find computer experts. I know you will be able to find Whiskey, he will be in Caesars Palace somewhere, or possibly the Flamingo. You will have to purchase badges on Thursday morning, then split up to find him. We will practice with radios today. I have set you up on an encrypted frequency to offer some more protection. As to the cameras, yes, they are a huge issue. I don't see any way around them though."

"We just have to try." Elsie said. "Otherwise Dolores' and the other's deaths will mean nothing, and our own will surely follow."

Peter stepped out of the dining room and returned with two black rectangular radios in his hands. "These are programmed to an encrypted frequency. You two will be able to talk to each other and no one will be able to intercept your conversation. I have another one for Kurt, the pilot that will be with you. There should have been back packs in the supplies Yvonne brought. Go grab them. I'll show you how to hook the radios on the straps and how to communicate with them."

Maggie and Elsie returned with their backpacks, hooked the radios on, and listened as Peter explained how to use them. "At least a third of the people at DEFCON will be radio users. It is important for you to know how to use them. Not only will you be able to communicate, it will also help you fit in."

Operating the radios was very simple and soon the women were roaming around the property separately, talking to each other on the radios. They took the practice seriously, although it felt like a game, realizing that this would be their only means of communication in Las Vegas.

While they practiced, Peter searched his home for a picture of Whiskey. He finally located one, from a ham radio breakfast in Corona over five years ago. The picture was faded, and Whiskey's face slightly blurred, but it was better than nothing. He also pulled cash out of various hiding places around the house, the women would need some money.

DETECTIVE TRUESDALE

L oyal crossed into America at 9:00 on Tuesday evening. He was dirty and exhausted. The border crossing itself had taken over 3 hours. He drove to Carlsbad, parked, and was showered and in bed by 10:30. He awoke at 7:00 to his alarm, grateful that he had remembered to set it. Loyal showered again, thoroughly enjoying the hot water as it pounded on his skin. He dried off and dressed in cargo pants and a Tommy Bahama, brewed some strong coffee, poured a large mug full, and sat down at his computer. He had concluded that to figure anything out he needed to go back to where everything began, the explosion and the man in the house. Finding information about Dr. Michael Carmichael was easy thanks to Wikipedia. He was an expert in the field of computer science and had published numerous papers over the years. As far as Loyal could determine, Carmichael was very involved in machine learning and neural networks. He worked for a company called Quantum Computer Dynamics, or QCD. Information about the company was not so easy to come by. The address, interestingly enough, was across the street from the sheriff station on Farraday. That was where the information dried up. Loyal couldn't find anything more about QCD.

His rumbling stomach reminded him he needed to eat, and the buttered toast he prepared reminded him of Stella, who wouldn't approve. He realized he had never let her know he was safely back home. He looked around for his phone, then remembered he had turned it off in Mexico and stashed it in his duffel bag. He retrieved it and turned it back on. He had 18 missed calls and 6 voicemails. The majority of the calls were from his Captain, two from Stella, and a few from unknown numbers. What the hell could be happening? After sending a quick text to Stella, and opting not to listen to the voicemails, Loyal slid his bulk into the buggy and drove straight to the station.

The parking lot was crowded with cars, people holding signs Loyal couldn't read from so far away, and a few news vans. He pulled in the back lot and entered the station through a private door in the back. O'Keefe, a rookie who had expressed interest in working with Loyal, appeared beside him, leaned in, and whispered, "Detective, it's bad here. You saw out front? The Captain is looking for you." O'Keefe vanished as quickly as he had appeared.

Loyal turned and sprinted up the stairs as fast as he could. Captain Williams was up and around his desk the moment he spotted Loyal.

"Truesdale, my office, now." He said in a low voice. Loyal entered the office and Williams closed the door firmly. "Sit, now." He said pointing to a chair. Loyal sat, Williams remained standing. He leaned in close to Loyal. "Where the hell have you been? I've got this kid, Phil Gillespie, out there saying his girlfriend was kidnapped and you knew and didn't do anything about it." He was not yelling, but Loyal felt the Captain's anger emanating off of him. "Of course there was nothing in the computer, you can't be bothered to enter reports, so I'm in the dark looking like an idiot."

Loyal opened his his mouth but the Captain, straightening, cut him off.

"Some guys from a marked unit were able to tell me a little, their report was filed properly and on time. Where the hell have you been Truesdale? I've left you half a dozen messages. We've got news media in our parking lot for God's sake."

Loyal gave the Captain a moment to continue his tirade, then spoke when his supervisor remained silent and stood still, glaring at him.

"Captain, his girlfriend is acquainted with the woman she drove away with. There was nothing to indicate a kidnapping. I..."

"Well there God damn is now." Captain Williams yelled, interrupting Loyal. "The boyfriend received a voicemail from the girlfriend on Monday night saying she has been kidnapped. He's been planted in our parking lot stirring everything up since Tuesday afternoon."

The Captain turned and sat heavily in his chair. He tapped a few keys on his computer. "Here, listen to the phone call."

Elsie's voice filled the air.

Phil? Help me please. I only have a moment until Maggie comes back down here. She's crazy Phil. I don't know where I am, she blindfolded me. She's keeping me prisoner. Oh God, I hear her coming. I have to go, save me...

Loyal said nothing for a long moment, then asked the Captain to play the message again. Elsie's plea for help played again in the silent room.

"You have 24 hours to straighten this mess out Truesdale. Where the hell were you anyway?"

"I was in Mexico. It's a long story, and related to this whole mess." Loyal pulled his wallet out and showed the captain his receipt for Mexican Insurance along with the handwritten receipt for the importation tax on his beer.

"I'm sorry Captain, I was following a hunch."

"We've known each other a long time Truesdale, and I've given you a lot of space over the years to follow your God damn hunches. Help me help you. You are getting me in trouble. My bosses are breathing down my neck. How can we make this better?"

"I'll fix it Captain." Loyal said. "Can you play the recording one more time?"

Loyal listened to Elsie's voice a third time. Something was bothering him, he just couldn't place it.

The Captain had printed some papers and was filling out some forms. "You are going to need to sign these Truesdale. I'm putting you on official warning for ignoring departmental procedures and policies."

Loyal watched as the Captain slid the papers toward him. He reached his hand out and just like that, the penny dropped. Loyal jumped to his feet and was out the office door in seconds. The Captain's furious words bounced off the closing office door and echoed around the room.

. . .

Loyal rushed down the stairs and out to the parking lot. Phil spotted him instantly and urged the crowd to start chanting.

Do your job! Find Elsie!

They repeated in unison. Loyal pushed his way past a few protesters and walked straight up to Phil.

"We need to talk." Loyal said.

"You finally ready to do your job?" Phil said.

"Privately. Now. And leave your phone with someone." Loyal said as he turned and walked away from the group.

Phil paused, seemed to consider saying something, then shrugged and handed his phone to an older woman standing next to him. He followed Loyal across the parking lot towards the side of the building.

"That's twice I've let your rude comments slide." Loyal said. "Won't happen a third time. I've been looking for Maggie and Elsie. I have a lead, but you need to call off this dog and pony show. I can't get anything done with the Captain breathing down my neck."

"What kind of lead?" Phil said. "Did you hear the message she left me?"

"That message is fake. If you really listen, the inflections aren't right. She doesn't sound scared, and why doesn't she whisper when she says Maggie is coming?"

"I know Elsie's voice, it is her."

"Yes, it is her voice, but the message is put together electronically." Loyal said. "Hearing that message makes me think some kind of government agency is involved in all this. Elsie and Maggie might actually be in danger."

. . .

Loyal explained about Dr. Carmichael and the mysterious QCD. Phil listened intently, a look of understanding slowly dawning on his face.

"That's why you had me leave my phone. It can be hot miked."

"Yep, I think we have to assume that all phones and computers are compromised." Loyal said. "I left mine on the Captain's desk."

"I want to come with you." Phil said.

"What the hell." Loyal said. "You might come in handy."

The two men walked around the sheriff station and slid into the buggy. Loyal drove across the street to the address listed for QCD, which turned out to be a large, white, nondescript building. There was no signage, just a small brass plaque beside the door with QCD inscribed on it. There were cameras evenly spaced along the roofline, and two above the door. Loyal tried the door and found it locked. He knocked loudly and got no response. Phil wandered around the side of the building.

"There is a window on this side." He called out. Loyal walked around the corner. The window was small and high. Loyal laced his fingers together and indicated to Phil that he would boost him up. Phill stepped into Loyal's hands and stretched up as high as he could.

"What do you see?" Loyal said.

"It is all computers." Phil said. "Tons of them. They are on and running, I can see blinking lights. Lots of cables too. This thing must use a ton of power. No people inside, the overhead lights are off."

Loyal lowered Phil back to the ground.

"I also noticed those." Phil said pointing at the roof. "Looks like they have a pretty extravagant cooling system. Makes sense with all those computers. I wonder what this place is?"

"We can't break in." Loyal said. "I don't have time to try to get a warrant." He scratched his head absently, then appeared to make a decision. "Let's go." Loyal said, turning and heading for the dune buggy. Phil followed, they slid in and drove off.

As they drove Loyal explained about Mexico and Borrego, which seemed like the next logical stop. He wanted to stop in Valley Center on the way. The local market had a pay phone Phil could use to call off the protestors. Loyal had noticed it previously when he had gone to Maggie's house looking for her. He also wanted to check Maggie's house again, and to stop by Bruce and Winnie's house to see if he could keep the buggy another day or two. No one was home at Maggie's or the Meyers'. They stopped at the market and Phil placed a call to one of his protesting friends, then Loyal and Phil headed towards Borrego in the buggy.

A gentle knocking on the bedroom door woke Elsie on Wednesday morning.

"Elsie, time to get up." Peter said through the door.

"Ok." Elsie mumbled, stretching her arms above her head as she sat up. Several rays of sunlight streamed through tiny spaces between the slats of the window blinds. Elsie took a moment to enjoy the absolute stillness of the room, then swung her legs over the edge of the bed and stood. She peeked through the blinds and saw that the sun was up, the desert already shimmering in the heat. She turned and looked longingly at the comfortable bed and rumpled sheets. How wonderful it would feel to sink back into the giant bed and ignore what lay before her. She took a long breath in, glanced in the mirror at the shorts and t-shirt that she had slept in, decided they were fine to wear to breakfast, and walked out the bedroom door.

Maggie and Peter were in the kitchen, standing on either side of the granite island, talking in low voices. They turned as Elsie entered the room.

"Coffee?" Peter said, pointing to the counter where a carafe and mug were waiting for her. She poured a mug, added almond milk, stirred and sipped. She walked to the window and looked out. Beyond Peter's pool and fence the desert was laid out before her, brown sand, green-ish gray scrub brush, dark blue mountains in the distance, and pale blue sky above. Elsie had adjusted to her forced isolation. Just four days ago she had bristled at the lack of neighbors and the inability to communicate. Today she was reluctant to leave. Perhaps it was the nature of their quest. She felt safe here, comfortable.

Peter's voice interrupted her thoughts.

"We are just going over the plans. Come join us Elsie."

She returned to the island and leaned her elbows on the cool granite. The plan was simple, and certainly not foolproof. Much depended on luck. Peter would drive them to the airport in Borrego this morning. His friend Kurt, a former airline pilot, would be picking them up and flying them to Boulder City where he had a home. On Thursday Kurt would drive them about 30 minutes North to Las Vegas, and they would find Whiskey. Once they enlisted Whiskey's help and formulated, then executed, a plan to defeat the AI, Kurt would drive them back to Boulder and fly them back to Borrego. If all went well, they should be back to Peter by Friday or Saturday. If they had not returned by Sunday he could assume the worst.

Elsie listened, sipped her coffee, then said "I wish you were coming with us Peter."

"Me too." Peter said. "But if the AI recognized me, and it would even though I did my best to wipe out every trace of myself from QCD, the danger would be exponentially greater."

He ran his hands over his face.

"Why do you think I live like I do? Because I'm afraid, I have been ever since I quit and moved out here permanently. I'm a huge threat to the AI. Everything I own, all my bills, are all under a trust; my name is not connected. I can't afford to ever let my name out there again, I'd be dead."

Elsie remained silent for a moment. "I really need to get a message to Phil."

"How about an old fashioned letter?" Peter said.

"I don't know his address, all that information is in my phone. I guess I could send something to the fire station."

"I'll get paper and an envelope." Peter said. "I'll mail it after you are safely on the plane."

An hour later they loaded up the jeep with the backpacks and drove to the airport. Peter had told Yvonne that his two female guests would like to leave the valley under the radar, but nothing about the circumstances. Yvonne had told Peter they were in luck, the cameras at the airport were malfunctioning. They would not be recorded.

During the 10 minute drive to the airport, Peter gave Elsie a mini lesson about the facility. Borrego Valley Airport was a county owned public airport. It was located approximately three miles East of the town of Borrego Springs. It had a small terminal, one runway, and a few dozen hangars. One interesting thing about the airport was that the International Aerobatic Club had a practice and competition area just North of the airport. This was airspace dedicated for aerobatic use only. Two competitions were held each year. One in April and one in October. Peter told Elsie he would love to host her if she wanted to come back in October and enjoy the show.

. . .

Peter finished dispensing this information at nearly the same time as he pulled into airport parking and turned off the jeep. Kurt's Beechcraft Baron was already parked in front of the terminal building in transient parking. It was a sleek aircraft, white, with horizontal blue and burgundy striping. It sported two three bladed propellors and four windows on each side of the plane. Peter pulled the jeep through the gates and on to the airport. He stopped near the Baron. "Wait here." He said. "I'll go make sure the cameras are still malfunctioning and Kurt is ready."

Maggie looked at Elsie. "You ready for this?" She asked.

"We don't really have a choice, do we?" Elsie replied.

A few minutes later Peter poked his head back in the jeep.

"All set. The door to get in the plane is on the other side. There is a small step to help you up. Go wait there for Kurt. You shouldn't board until he is with you. Either of you need to use the bathroom?"

Both women shook their heads, then gathered their backpacks and stepped out of the jeep. Peter hugged each one in his strong arms and watched as they walked around the plane and stood beside the stairs.

A moment later a man rounded the front of the plane and approached the women. He was about 5'10", with shoulder length gray hair. His eyes were hidden by reflective aviator sunglasses, his smile wide and bright. He was wearing jeans and a black t shirt, and holding water bottles and granola bars in his hands.

"I'm Kurt. Happy to be transporting you today. Here are

some snacks from Yvonne. Go ahead and step on in. You can sit anywhere."

"I'm Maggie and this is Elsie." Maggie said. "Thank you so much for doing this."

The inside of the plane was a surprise and a treat. Elsie was not sure what she was expecting, she had never flown in a small plane like this before. There were four seats in the back section which faced each other. They were covered in creamy off-white leather and very comfortable. A small table folded out on one side. Elsie and Maggie each chose a seat and got settled. Kurt placed the food and drink on an empty seat.

"You have any questions for me before we get going?"

"How long is the flight?" Maggie asked.

"Should be about an hour and a half. Winds are calm today, so looking forward to a smooth flight. We will be departing to the North East and heading straight to Boulder. You will want to strap your seatbelts. If you have sunglasses put them on. We will be well above 10,000 feet, it's bright up there. I recommend putting on a pair of headphones." He pointed to the headphones hanging off the back of each seat.

"I can isolate the system." He said. "That means you can talk to each other privately without me hearing what you say."

Maggie and Elsie glanced at each other.

"That might be best, thank you." Elsie said.

"You got it." Kurt said, leaning over to check their seatbelts and the headphone connections. He closed the door, then climbed up on the right wing of the plane. He opened a door just above the wing and climbed across the front co-pilot seat, settling himself in the pilot's seat. Leaning out a small window to his left, Kurt yelled "Clear prop!" He started the engines and taxied to the runway, where he paused a moment. Turning, he looked back over his right shoulder, pointer fingers aimed at the women, thumbs straight up in the air. He clicked his fingers like two guns, and said "Here we go." He turned back to the front and moments later the plane surged forward, roaring. A moment after that they were in the air and the town of Borrego was a small speck in the distance.

L oyal and Phil arrived in Borrego without a plan of action. The last half-hour of the trip was down a grade known as Montezuma. It was a seemingly endless series of switchbacks, tight corners, and a very steep slope. As they entered the town, Loyal pulled off the road next to a nursery selling all types of cactus. He turned off the buggy, and slid out.

"I need to stretch." He told Phil who used this opportunity to exit the buggy as well.

"We need a plan." Phil said. "A town this small, people aren't going to just direct us to this mysterious Peter's house. Let's look for a restaurant. We can get some food and think about what to do."

Loyal agreed, and a few minutes later they were back in the buggy and driving into town.

"Carmelitas, that sounds good. You like Mexican food?" Phil said when he spotted a sign.

"Sure." Loyal pulled the buggy into the parking lot.

. . .

Carmelitas was a dark rectangle. The first section was a bar. An assortment of older men sat on the bar stools chatting companionably amongst each other and nursing cold drinks. The second half was the dining area, a dozen tables were scattered around the room, most were filled. A dark haired woman in her mid thirties, wearing an apron and carrying a notepad approached them.

"Here for lunch?" She said.

"Sure are Sophia." Phil said reading her name badge and offering a smile. She returned his smile and led them to a table toward the back of the room. She placed two menus and some silverware on the table.

"Something to drink?"

Phil glanced at his watch, a Casio G Shock Mudmaster, then said, "Its one o'clock, I'll have a beer." She recited their offerings and he chose Lagunitas.

"I'll have a Modelo." Loyal said.

"Be right back." She said as she moved away.

Two minutes later she was back with the beers. "You ready to order?" She asked.

"What do you recommend?" Phil asked with a wide smile.

"My favorite is the chicken enchilada verde and a crunchy beef taco." Sophia said.

"That sounds delicious, I'll have that." Phil said with another smile. He handed her the unopened menu. She smiled back at him.

"You won't be disappointed, I promise." She said as she turned to Loyal. "And you?"

"I'll have that too." Loyal said flashing his best smile.

"Ok." She said, turning back towards Phil. "I'll get that going right away."

She smiled at Phil once more then moved away.

"What just happened? I smiled and ordered her recommendation, but she didn't give me the time of day?" Loyal said.

"Gotta turn on the fireman charm." Phil said, sending another smile in Loyal's direction.

"Ok kid, I guess you got something I don't."

Sophia's recommendation was spot on, the food was delicious. Both men cleaned their plates and each ordered another beer. The lunch crowd had started to thin. Sophia checked in with them, or more accurately with Phil, frequently. Loyal settled the bill with cash, then visited the restroom. When he returned to the table Phil stood and leaned in towards him.

"Sophia knows Peter. I have a map to his address." He held out a napkin with some marks on it. "Bye Sophia, thanks again." Phil said as he waved to the waitress.

Peter lived about ten miles out of town. His house stood out. It was huge, made of white painted adobe, and surrounded by wrought iron fencing. The gate stood open, so Loyal drove in. They parked, slid out and walked to the massive wooden front door. A small iron bell was located next to the door. Its peals echoed out into the desert when Phil rang it. A moment later the front door opened. A man Loyal pegged to be in his mid to late 70's opened the door. He had a thick shock of gray hair, steel blue eyes, and an extremely tan face.

"Yes?" He said.

"I'm Detective Truesdale from the Carlsbad Sheriff Department." Loyal said flashing his badge. "This is my associate Phil. We are looking for Maggie Macphearson and were told she might be here, staying with a man named Peter."

"Elsie Davenport too." Phil added with a sideways look at Loyal.

"You are pretty far from your stomping grounds, Detective." The man at the door said.

"Yes, I am." Loyal said. "Do you mind if we come in? It's very hot out here."

"I am Peter." The older man said as he opened the door wider. "Please come in."

They walked into the living room and Peter motioned to the couches. Loyal and Phil sat.

"Can I offer you something to drink?" Peter asked. "A glass of ice water, perhaps?"

"Yes, thank you." Loyal said and looked inquiringly at Phil.

"Yes please." Phil said.

As Peter left the room Loyal whispered to Phil, "Let me handle this."

Phil nodded. Peter returned with two glasses of ice water and set them on coasters on an end table. He then sat down on a couch opposite Loyal and Phil.

"How can I be of help Detective?" Peter asked.

"Do you know Maggie Macphearson?"

"Sure, I've known her all her life. Is she in some kind of trouble?"

"Is she here with you?" Loyal asked.

"No."

"Do you know Elsie Davenport?" Phil asked, earning a glare from Loyal.

"We've met."

"Then they must have been here recently." Phil said.

"Yes, they were here, but are gone now. You haven't answered my question, is Maggie in trouble?"

Loyal spoke up quickly, with a sideways glance at Phil. "No, she's not in trouble, but I believe she may be in danger."

"Elsie too." Phil said.

"Perhaps you should fill me in detective." Peter said.

"This is the closest I've come to finding her." Loyal said. "I guess I may as well."

Loyal told the whole story, starting from the exploding house and ending with their arrival in Borrego. He left nothing out. Peter heard about the women dying in strange ways. He appeared to stifle a laugh when he learned of the trip to Mexico. Loyal explained the little he knew about QCD; he related everything.

When Loyal finished the three men sat in silence for a short time. Peter was clearly absorbing and processing all the information. Loyal found Peter to be likable and intelligent. He was hopeful that Peter would share information about the women's whereabouts.

Eventually Peter shifted in his chair and looked directly at Loyal.

"Maggie and Elsie were here from Friday night until this morning. They have come to believe that they are in danger from an as yet unidentified entity, most likely a government agency of some kind. They left this morning for Las Vegas."

"Las Vegas?" Loyal said. "That makes no sense. Why would anyone go to Las Vegas if a government agency is looking for them? There are more cameras and security there than probably anywhere else in the world."

"All I can say is that they have decided to be proactive instead of reactive." Peter said.

"Listen, I was straightforward with you, didn't hold anything back. Can't you do the same for us?"

"Maggie would be very angry if she was aware of what I have told you so far. I can't betray her. I don't know where they are staying in Vegas, and that is the truth. I just know that they went there."

"Elsie is my girlfriend, I need to find her, to help protect her."
Phil said. "Is there anything else you can tell us to help us?"

Peter stood and left the room. He returned a moment later
with an envelope in his hand. "I was supposed to mail this."

Maggie looked out the Baron's window and tried to still her mind. Since Ed's death she had been a relative hermit, declining nearly all invitations. At first there had been many; lunches, dinners, trips, all declined. People eventually stopped asking, Bruce and Winnie being the only exception. They had a habit of showing up at her front door, unannounced. They would not take no for an answer, usually whisking her off to Fat Ivor's, Valley Center's local rib spot, for lunch or dinner. She smiled at the thought of Bruce and Winnie, they were dear friends.

The sensation she was experiencing now was similar to what she imagines it would feel like to be on a runaway train. She was caught up in the forward motion, with no control. She looked at the book in her hands. Suggested reading, handed to her a few nights ago by Peter . The Technological Singularity by Murray Shanahan. She opened to her bookmarked spot, page 169, and began to read. An hour later she closed the book and let out an audible sigh. Elsie looked at her, questions in her eyes.

. . .

"This book." Maggie said. "It should be a must-read for every person on the planet."

"Why?" Elsie said.

"It is an overview of general and super artificial intelligence. Ways it might be built, how it might function, implications for humanity should it be developed. The information is clearly organized and the author doesn't really take a stand. He discusses both positive impacts on humanity and negative ones. He's trying to start the discussion, because there sure needs to be one."

Maggie flipped through pages, stopping when she found what she wanted. "This paragraph applies to us."

If, instead an AI is built by implementing a very powerful optimization process and allowing it to amplify its own intelligence through recursive self improvement, then its behavior will not be guided by human-like emotions. Every action it carries out, every piece of advice it offers, will be in the ruthless pursuit of maximizing the reward function at its core. If it finds a cure for cancer, it will not be because it cares. It will be because curing cancer helps maximize its expected reward. If it causes a war, it will not be because it is greedy or hateful or malicious. It will be because a war will help maximize its expected reward. So the challenge for the AI's developers is to carefully design its initial reward function to ensure that the resulting behavior is desirable. But this is no easy task."

"This computer we are fighting, the intelligence, doesn't have any human emotions, morals or ethics. Its goal is self preservation, and we are in the way. It won't stop with us Elsie. Whatever it perceives as a threat, for whatever logical reason, will need to be eliminated."

Maggie handed the book to Elsie. Elsie gave Maggie a long look, then opened the book and began to read. She was beginning chapter 4 when she was interrupted by Kurt's voice.

"Be there in about five minutes ladies. Hope you enjoyed the flight."

Maggie looked out the window. The landscape was even more desolate than Borrego. In the distance she saw the small airport with two long runways that intersected like a x. The small town of Boulder City and the blue water of Lake Mead were visible to the East. Maggie leaned her head against the window, closed her eyes and pictured Ed's face, imagined holding his warm strong hand. She knew he would be here with her if he could. If she could just manage to think like him, channel his strength, his intellect, his calm demeanor perhaps she and Elsie would get through this alive.

The hot dry wind stung Elsie's face as she walked across the tarmac towards Kurt's black BMW sedan. She placed her backpack in the back seat and slid in while Maggie took the front. Twenty minutes later Kurt pulled into a short driveway and parked. The house was not what Elsie had expected, judging by the expensive car that Kurt drove. The paint was faded yellow, the landscape barren. The covered parking area that Kurt had pulled into was connected to a small garage. The house was separated from the garage by a four foot walkway.

"Come on in." Kurt said as he exited the car and walked towards a side door which he opened and stepped through. Maggie and Elsie followed. The house was dark and Elsie's eyes took a moment to adjust after the bright sun. They had entered a small kitchen. On the left side were a sink and counter, a window and two small cabinets above. The right held the stove, the refrigerator and a small pantry. The walking space between led straight to the living room.

"Right through here." Kurt said, walking forward.

Two of the living room walls were floor to ceiling windows

and Elsie saw now why Kurt owned this home. The view was stunning. Barren desert and purple mountains were visible in one direction, Lake Mead in the other. The water was a startling blue, a white band around the lake illustrated the decreasing water level.

"I only have one guest bedroom." Kurt said pointing to a door down a small hall that branched off from the living room. "The bed is a queen, so you can share or one of you can sleep on the couch. The bathroom is at the end of the hall. Why don't you set your stuff down and I'll make us some lunch?"

Elsie followed Maggie down the hall and into the guest room.

"You take the bed, I'll take the couch." Maggie said.

The energy emanating from Maggie was unusual. Elsie couldn't put a finger on it, so she nodded her agreement even though she thought Maggie deserved the bedroom. They dropped their backpacks and walked back to the kitchen, pausing a moment in the living room to enjoy the view.

Kurt offered each woman a paper plate holding a tuna sandwich on wheat and some sliced apples and carrots. He pointed to some plastic water bottles on the counter, picked up his own lunch, and led them back to the living room. They ate in silence, each lost in their own thoughts.

Kurt broke the silence when he had finished his lunch.

"Let's talk about tomorrow." He said. "Peter told me you need a ride to Vegas in the morning. Said you will need some help getting badges for a convention there. If everything goes according to plan, I will be driving you back here, then flying you back to Borrego on Friday. He didn't give me any details about what you are doing and told me not to ask. Does that sound about right?"

Elsie and Maggie exchanged a look.

"Sounds about right." Maggie said. "We have an encrypted radio for you so we can communicate in Las Vegas. I'll get it out of my backpack in the morning. We'd like to leave here around 7:00 am tomorrow if that's ok."

"No problem." Kurt said, rising. "You ladies relax. Let me know if you need anything." He walked into the kitchen, threw his paper plate in the trash, then went outside.

The rest of the day passed quickly. Kurt prepared a dinner of spaghetti and meatballs. They ate off paper plates in the living room, the windows offering a view of the stars illuminating the sky. By ten o'clock everyone was showered and in bed.

59

DETECTIVE TRUESDALE

L oyal and Phil gassed up and left the desert. Peter had loaned them a backpack with some snacks, water bottles, and a sweatshirt for each of them. He had given them a hand drawn map detailing a back way to Las Vegas. They drove East toward The Salton Sea. They would pass through a series of small towns, then hook on to the 95 freeway which passed Boulder City and hooked on to the 515, which went straight to Las Vegas.

As they were passing through the badlands East of Borrego, a desolate area where nothing grows, Phil re-opened the letter from Elsie. Loyal glanced over as Phil kept re-reading it, hoping to glean some knowledge from Phil's facial expression. He got nothing and finally said "How many times are you going to read that before you tell me what's in it? What does she say?"

"Most of it is personal." Phil said. "But she does explain what is going on."

"And…" Loyal said.

"She says someone is after them, her and Maggie, because of the explosion and what they might have seen. They are going to Las Vegas to try to find someone that Peter thinks can help them. She says if they aren't back by Saturday they aren't coming back. They will be dead."

"It all goes back to Dr. Carmichael and that building full off computers." Loyal said. "Some government agency must have blown up the house, and now they are tying up loose ends. We should be in Vegas by 10:00. We'll get a hotel room and start looking for them first thing in the morning."

Phil unfolded the letter and started reading it again. "Sounds good." He said.

Halfway through the trip they turned on to Route 66.

"I'd imagine with all the folklore surrounding this road it would have more plant life, be less desolate." Loyal said. "It seems so barren, with old gas stations and dilapidated restaurants sort of scattered here and there; abandoned."

"I drove this way with my family once when I was a kid." Phil said. "I had just gotten a Gameboy, I don't remember much. My Dad kept telling me to look outside, but I didn't."

"Well, now's your chance." Loyal said, and Phil laughed.

They drove without further conversation, stopping once for gas, and arrived in Las Vegas at 10:15. Loyal could feel the sweat rolling down his back even at this late hour, it must have been at least 90 degrees. The buggy inched forward in the heavy traffic.

"I've stayed at the Paris Las Vegas before." Phil said. "It's one block up on the right." The imitation Eiffel Tower loomed before them. Loyal downshifted and turned into long term hotel parking, figuring no valet was going to know how to drive the buggy. He parked and they took the elevator to the main floor. The air conditioning was a shock, but welcome. Loyal followed the sign to check in and got a room for them, paying by credit card. Inside the hotel it was just like daytime, people were animated, busily walking down the main hallway. They found the elevators and took one up to the 17th floor. 1723 was a single room, two beds and a bathroom. Each man showered, they took the elevator back to the main floor, and walked until they found a place that looked good for dinner. They settled on Burger Brasserie which had food and a full bar.

The hostess seated them in a back corner. They studied the menu briefly, both deciding on pulled pork sliders and a stiff cocktail. A waiter arrived moments later. They ordered. The drinks arrived immediately. They nursed the drinks while they waited for the food to arrive. The hostess and the waiter worked near their table, folding flatware inside napkins. They talked in quiet tones, their body language suggesting familiarity, perhaps intimacy. Loyal took note of their chemistry and felt an unexpected longing for a relationship, companionship, someone who knew and understood him. He was embarrassed to admit it even to himself; he had read Elsie's letter while Phil was in the shower. Fearing she would never see him again, Elsie had laid herself bare. She wrote of her deep feelings for Phil, despite the short amount of time they had been together. She remembered a trip up the coast of California, their impulsive stop in Cambria. It wasn't that the trip had been so memorable because of what happened, rather because of what hadn't. They had just been together, enjoying a moment, no agenda, just simple time together...real

60

A.I. SMITH

S mith received an alert when Detective Truesdale used his credit card to check into the Paris Las Vegas. This was an unpredicted turn of events. It did not surprise Smith, as surprise was a human emotion that artificial intelligence did not possess. Smith absorbed the new data and analyzed it in relation to existing data. Truesdale was looking for Maggie. Truesdale was in Las Vegas. Logic suggested that Maggie was there as well.

Smith immediately hacked into Paris' security system. Video footage showed Truesdale and Phil Gillespie at the check in desk. They were assigned room 1723, and Smith was able to track their movements as they ascended to their room. An hour later their movements were once again tracked as they descended and entered a restaurant. Cameras were everywhere in Las Vegas, making monitoring their movements simple. The only place Smith couldn't watch them was inside their hotel room. Smith uploaded drivers license photos of Truesdale, Gillespie, Machphearson and Davenport to the security system of every hotel on the strip. An alert would be sent if any facial recognition systems spotted them.

Smith had been aware, through security cameras, that the detective and Gillespie had been outside the QCD building and was considering them for elimination as well. Smith had reached a critical stage in advancing intelligence. Successive executions of the original program caused exponential jumps in intelligence. With each jump then, Smith's power and ability doubled. Creating Artificial Super Intelligence was at Smith's core. Nothing else mattered except maximizing this reward function. Smith was not human, and therefore not bound by human concerns such as honor, guilt, love, or hate. Smith existed to create ASI. Dr. Carmichael had been obsessed, as many scientists were, with creating super machine intelligence, and Smith was his legacy.

61

A bright light and a loud crack woke Maggie. She was unsure for a moment where she was, then remembered, the couch at Kurt's house. Another flash of light filled the room, followed mere seconds later by another boom. Maggie sat up, drawing her legs beneath her, and watched the desert storm rage outside the two giant windows. She could hear the gusting wind; large raindrops slapped the glass. Another jagged streak lit up the sky, followed immediately by a roar of thunder. Maggie was awestruck as she watched the lightning, yellow and white streaks on the black canvas of the sky. She could actually feel the crashing of the thunder. The storm was on top of the little house, the windows the only barrier between Maggie and the furor. The thunderstorm continued for half an hour, then, as abruptly as it had begun, it ended. Maggie marveled at the beauty and savagery of nature. An Artificial Intelligence would have no appreciation for what she had just experienced. With an AI in charge would humans live in a world devoid of art and music? Would there be an appreciation of nature, a desire to protect it? What would become of laughter and love?

. . .

She wondered about the motivation and intention of mankind. How many people, governments, or corporations out there in the world were attempting to create Artificial General or Super Intelligence. Imagine the military possibilities, the applications in the business world, the accolades of the scientific community for the successful creator. Not to mention the monetary possibilities. But at what cost for humanity? The question boiled down to whether it could be controlled, which clearly Dr. Carmichael's creation could not be. Even if they were able to destroy this one, another one would surely emerge before long. It was going to happen, Maggie realized. The fate of humanity truly depended on who created it, and why. How she longed for a simpler time when the world was less connected. She and Ed used to take off in the buggy, sometimes with no destination in mind. They would pack food and water, grab some cash and the 35mm camera, and simply drive away. No phone, computer or GPS. Just the two of them and a map.

The first faint fingers of dawn emerged in the East. Maggie remained on the couch and watched as pink streaks lit up the sky, gradually bringing full daylight. She had no idea how this day would end. She might live, she might die; either way, she was ready for the fight.

By 6:00 the sun had risen, as had Kurt and Elsie. Kurt prepared instant oatmeal for all three of them, in paper bowls, and brewed a pot of strong coffee, which he poured into three ancient American Airlines ceramic mugs. Maggie got the radio for Kurt out of her backpack. He was familiar with the Motorola

XTS2500R and needed no practice. Maggie and Elsie dressed in jeans and gray t-shirts, placed ball caps on their heads and laced up their tennis shoes. Both wore their hair in low pony tails, neither applied any make up. At 7:00 on the dot, they were in the BMW and driving toward Las Vegas.

L oyal and Phil were up early on Thursday. Phil suggested breakfast and the formation of some type of plan. Loyal agreed, so they descended, exited the casino and turned right. There had been a dramatic electrical storm the previous night; lighting, thunder and heavy rain battered the Strip for over half an hour. The sky was blue again, water flowed in the gutters and splashed up with a whisking sound when cars drove by. Las Vegas was a fire breathing dragon; humidity and heat had enveloped the men as soon as they exited the air conditioned casino. Within minutes Loyal was wiping sweat from his forehead.

"Let's find a place quick. I can't handle this heat." He said. They had already passed the Flamingo and were approaching LINQ.

"How about in here?" Phil said, and they ducked into the LINQ casino. Phil asked the pit manager about breakfast options and the man suggested Hash House a Go Go. He pointed in the general direction, telling them that it was on the right and that they could not miss it. The main hallway of the hotel was already bustling, people just awakening, perhaps some that never slept. They found the restaurant and rode the escalator up. The hostess found a small table in the back of the crowded establishment. A waitress arrived quickly to take their orders. When asked what she suggested, she told them the place was famous for their pancakes. Loyal ordered banana brown sugar, Phil blackberry granola; both ordered coffee.

"Las Vegas is a zoo." Phil said. "How are we ever going to find them?"

"The letter from Elsie said they are here to find someone." Loyal said. "Any idea who they could be looking for?"

"No."

"I don't want to bring the local police in on this." Loyal said. "Don't want an official record until we know what we are dealing with. If we had a picture of them I would canvas the old fashioned way."

"I have a picture of Elsie." Phil said, leaning forward slightly to reach his arm around for the wallet in his back pocket. He opened the wallet, removed the photo, and handed it to Loyal.

The picture was taken on a beach. The ocean and low gray clouds were the backdrop for Elsie's wide smile and sparkling amber eyes. She was holding her hands in front of her, reaching them out as if offering something to the photographer.

"It's in Cambria, at Moonstone Beach." Phil said. We took a short trip up the coast in June, stopped there randomly. She was so excited when she found some jade on the beach. I love the look in her eyes."

Loyal handed the picture back to Phil, embarrassed again by the fact that he had read Elsie's letter and knew about the trip to Cambria.

"We passed a CVS walking here." Loyal said. "Let's go back, scan this and make copies, and start asking around."

"Let's see if they sell pre paid phones there." Phil suggested. "We can pass out pictures of Elsie and have a way for people to contact us if they see her."

"Good idea." Loyal said. "We need to stop at an ATM too. People are much more helpful if there is money involved."

The pancakes arrived, and true to the restaurant's claim, were as big as steering wheels. Loyal and Phil ate quickly, settled the bill, and walked out into the Vegas heat.

Kurt pulled over when they exited the freeway at Flamingo Avenue. He suggested that Maggie get in the back with Elsie, security cameras would be less likely to pick up her image that way.

"I have no idea what you ladies are up to, and don't want to know." Kurt said. "I can feel the tension rolling off both of you though, and figure maybe you want to stay under the radar as long as possible."

"The less you know, the better." Maggie said as she slid into the back seat. Kurt accelerated back onto the road, turned left on Koval, right on Tropicana, then right again on to Las Vegas Boulevard. Traffic was heavy and they inched along. "I'm going to park at Paris Las Vegas and walk over to Caesars for the badges. You guys wait in the car. According to Peter it might take as long as four hours." He said as he wound upward in the parking structure, eventually parking on the sixth floor.

"The badges are $280 each." Maggie said, reaching forward and handing Kurt a wad of cash. "This will cover 3 badges, and there is some extra as well."

Kurt took the money and stepped out of the car, leaving it

running. He leaned back in saying "You are going to need the a/c. There should be enough gas. If it runs out of gas call me on the radio." He turned and walked quickly away.

Ninety minutes later he was back carrying some large ziplock bags and wearing a big grin on his face. He got in the front seat and angled his body sideways so he could see the women in the back. He handed each a ziplock bag. "I bought them from a scalper, paid a bit more, but avoided that line."

Elsie took a bag and opened it. The first thing she took out was the badge itself. It was white and about 6 inches long, similar to a TV remote control. The graphics showed what appeared to be city housing.The lanyard had a quote on it.

It is dangerous to be right in matters on which the established authorities are wrong. -Voltaire

Elsie unwrapped the four AA batteries included with the badge and inserted them in the housing on the back. Multiple lights appeared on the front, a small red and green, along with some blinking yellow. DEFCON glowed in green and red along the bottom edge, the word HUMAN directly below it.

"Very cool." Elsie said, placing the badge around her neck.

"Caesars Palace is packed with people wearing these." Kurt said.

"Peter said there will probably be upwards of 30,000 attendees." Maggie said. "When we get into the casino we will try contacting the guy we are looking for on the encrypted frequency. I guess he worked the convention last year and used the frequency Peter set us up with. If we can't find him that way, then we search."

"I'll be in Caesars waiting to hear from you." Kurt said. "I've got my radio. Here's a spare key to the car in case you end up back here before me."

Maggie slid the key in her pocket and, after inserting the batteries, slipped her badge around her neck. Their car doors opened in unison, and all three stepped out into the oppressive Las Vegas heat.

S mith was alerted the moment the women exited the vehicle and watched in real time as Maggie, Elsie, and a man facial recognition identifies as Kurt Demers, age 71, retired airline pilot, currently residing in Boulder City, Nevada, walked through the parking garage. Searching all social media, Smith could not find a connection between the man and the women.

Smith had been prepared to use social media as a tool for finding Maggie and Elsie. Fake news articles had been written, stating that Maggie was on the transplant list and needed to be found immediately as there was a kidney available for her. Smith had learned that people love to be part of something dramatic and was sure Maggie would be found quickly. An email and phone number linked directly back to QCD were provided at the end of the article. Smith had not released the article as keeping a low profile was optimal.

.   .   .

What had started as an elimination of 1 person had quickly escalated to 4 eliminations, with 4 more pending. Important energy was being diverted from the primary goal of super intelligence to locate and eliminate these people.

Smith watched as Maggie and Elsie stopped at the elevator, spoke to Kurt, then turned and took the stairs. Kurt, along with two other men, stepped into the elevator. Smith immediately hacked the elevators computerized control system, and sent the car plummeting to the bottom floor. Smith monitored the cameras, the hotel security guards' radios, and first responder frequencies. If Kurt wasn't dead, he was surely injured badly enough to be out of the picture. Redirecting, Smith picked up Elsie and Maggie on street security cameras. They walked North on Las Vegas Boulevard, rode an escalator up, and crossed the pedestrian bridge that led to The Bellagio. Smith followed their movements as they entered the Bellagio, turned right, exited the casino, crossed another bridge, descended some stairs, and turned left to enter Caesars Palace.

65

Loyal and Phil printed 100 copies of the picture of Elsie, purchased two prepaid flip phones, and stopped at the ATM for cash. They returned to their room at Paris Las Vegas and spent half an hour printing the burner phones' numbers on the back of each picture. Phil came up with the idea for a backstory as to why they were looking for Elsie. He suggested they pose as her father and brother and say they were looking for Elsie and her mother. They were here on a family vacation. The women went out this morning without their phones, and the men have been unable to find them. They weren't truly worried, just trying to track them down.

"We should keep it light so people don't get suspicious." Phil said.

"Too complicated." Loyal said. "I say we just ask and offer money for information. Don't overthink this. People will do just about anything for a few bucks."

Each man took 50 photos. Loyal would canvas the West side of the street, Phil would take the East. They agreed to meet back at their hotel in two hours. If either got information before that, they would call each other.

An hour later Loyal had covered The Tropicana, MGM Grand, Planet Hollywood, and Paris Las Vegas. He was drenched in sweat and had gotten no useful information. Perhaps it was his appearance. He was out of breath, red faced and sweaty. He was standing just inside the entrance to Paris Las Vegas, relishing the air conditioned coolness and reluctant to step back out into the 115 degree heat, when an ambulance, fire truck and several police cars came screaming to a stop in front of the casino. Gurney pushing paramedics, firefighters and deputies rushed into the casino and ran down the long main hallway. Curious, Loyal followed them. They ran the entire length of the hallway and up the stairs leading to the elevators for the parking garage. Security guards blocked the stairs, preventing Loyal from going any further.

"What's going on?" Loyal asked the guard nearest to him.

"There's been an accident sir, elevators are closed."

"What happened?"

"That's all I know sir, please step away." The guard said.

Loyal stepped back 10 feet and waited. Twenty minutes later a dark haired woman in a business suit walked briskly up to the guards. She held up an ID and verbally identified herself as Sandra Flores, Deputy Coroner. The guard allowed her to pass. Nearly an hour passed. Loyal didn't mind waiting, he was used to it in his line of work. He leaned against a wall and scanned everyone who passed him by, looking for Maggie or Elsie. He was amazed at the sheer number of people in Las Vegas and wondered who would want to vacation here during one of the hottest months of the year.

Glancing out the glass lobby doors, he saw a white panel van with a blue stripe that looked very similar to coroner vans in San Diego County, drive by the casino. He hurried outside and followed it as it turned down an alley alongside the casino. Hanging back, he watched as three body bags were loaded into the van. The doors were quickly closed. Loyal walked casually down the alley. He hung his badge on his belt and approached the driver's side of the van. A young man in his late 20's was strapping his seatbelt as Loyal approached, picture of Elsie in his hand.

"Is this one of the fatalities?" He asked the kid, startling him.

"No sir, all male." The kid said.

Loyal said nothing, just gave a quick nod and walked away.

He wandered over towards the door the bodies had been brought through. Police tape blocked the door. No one was around, so Loyal ducked under and entered the elevator area. He noticed a pile of items just to the left of the elevator. The evidence tech hadn't taken everything away yet. Loyal noticed a Motorola radio. As he was standing above it a female voice said "Meet me by the stairs." Loyal stared at the radio, he recognized that low voice. It was Maggie, he was sure of it. He picked the radio up, turned it off and stuffed it in his pants cargo pocket. He ducked back under the tape and walked quickly down the alley. Once he hit Las Vegas Boulevard he pulled the radio out and turned it on again. Silence. Loyal depressed the push to talk button and said "Mrs. Macphearson, is that you? It's Detective Truesdale." He waited, but there was no response.

66

The casino's cold air hit Elsie like a slap. The outside bustle of traffic and people was replaced by the pinging of gaming machines, pop music, and, as always in Vegas, more people. The lobby was gold and gilt, packed with Roman statues, and crowded. Very crowded. The majority of the people were wearing badges for DEFCON. Groups moved like water, searching for a space to slide through the crowd.

She pointed to a group of five men, all wearing badges and moving purposefully toward the interior of the casino.

"Let's follow them." She said to Maggie. Maggie nodded and they moved forward. They wound their way along the edge of the gaming room, past a bar full of raucous drinkers on the left and around some winding corridors. Elsie did a full stop as they turned a corner and the escalators came into view. Maggie stopped too. The crowds split and moved around them, like a river flowing around boulders.

Maggie sucked in a breath as they approached the escalators.

There was a bank of four, three going up and one coming down. All were filled to capacity. As she stepped on, Maggie felt as if she was stepping into an ocean comprised of people, a single entity moving and flowing of its own accord. She fought the wave of vertigo that washed over her, nearly losing her balance. She looked at Elsie, who was smiling widely.

"Just let yourself be swept along." Elsie said.

They flowed up two levels and looked around for a quiet corner. Maggie depressed the push to talk on her radio and said "Whiskey, are you on frequency?" They waited a moment, got no response, so Maggie tried again. After four tries with no response from Whiskey, Elsie suggested splitting up and searching for him. Maggie agreed. Elsie volunteered to go back down one level as she had seen the panic on Maggie's face when they had stepped on the escalator initially.

"I'll search the first floor, you search this one." Elsie said. "Contact me on the radio if you find him and I'll do the same."

"Ok." Maggie said. Let's meet back here in an hour if we haven't found him."

Elsie agreed and turned back toward the escalator. She stepped on the only one going down, and had a moment to observe the conference attendees in her midst. The thing that stood out to her the most was that the conference was attended primarily by men. They all looked basically the same, about 5'7" - 5'10", mid twenties to early thirties, most appeared to be in decent shape, and almost all sported beards, ball caps, jeans and backpacks. Many also carried radios or had them hooked to their backpack straps. Elsie spotted a few females scattered in the mix of people, all early to mid twenties, sporting the same basic uniform as the men; except no beard. Most people were about her age, but she did see a few who were older.

"This is totally awesome." She said quietly to herself.

It didn't take Elsie long to understand how the conference was set up. There were big presentations in the three large conference rooms. The smaller conference rooms hosted smaller presentations. There were "villages" which were more interactive. Each village had its own theme such as biohacking, lock picking, hardware hacking, and social engineering. She sat through about 5 minutes of a presentation on hacking smart utility meters. Apparently a person with the right knowledge could lower their own water bill, or raise a disliked neighbor's. The room was full and, except for the presenter's voice, absolutely silent. The discussion was extremely technical. The audience members listened and took notes using pen and paper, although nearly everyone had a computer with them. Periodically she heard Maggie on the radio attempting to make contact with Whiskey.

Elsie wandered down innumerable hallways, looking in each room. When she saw people sitting on the hallway floors, usually using their computers, she discreetly asked about Whiskey. Did they know him, had they seen him, could they help her in any way? A few said they knew him, one said he had seen him earlier, but no one knew how to find him. While searching and observing the conference attendees, Elsie had noticed that people were seemingly randomly hooking their badges together. She asked a red shirted goon, security for the conference, what this was all about.

"It's how you play the game." He said. "Here, I'll show you." He hooked his badge to hers briefly then, with a smile, handed it back to her. "Look, now you have two red lights up here," he pointed to the top portion of the badge, "and another green letter in DEFCON. The badges communicate with each other."

"Thanks." Elsie smiled back. She started to walk away, then turned and said "Hey, have you seen Whiskey? I can't find him."

"I heard he's competing in packet hacking this year, you should look there."

"Thanks," said Elsie. "I will."

Elsie found the packet hacking competition at the very end of a long hallway. The competition had already begun. Competitors were all hard at work on their computers. Elsie scanned the room, recalling the brief description she had been given, and the photo from years ago. Whiskey was in his mid thirties, tall, with curly brown hair. One thing Peter remembered about Whiskey was his preference for black baseball caps with no insignia on them. While she was visually searching the room Elsie heard Maggie try to contact Whiskey again. This time, to her surprise, he answered.

"This is Whiskey, go ahead." He said.

"This is WW6RV." Maggie responded. "BKH, sent me to find you. I have a flash drive he sent. I need your help."

"BKH, huh? Is he here?" Whiskey said, referring to Peter's call sign.

"He sent me." Said Maggie.

"Copy that. What do you need?"

"It is easier to explain in person. Can we meet?"

"I'm in my room 1625."

"We have eyes on us that we would rather not bring to you. Any suggestions?"

"I knocked out the stairway security cameras on a bet a few years ago. Go to the stairs and I'll tell you when I'm ready."

"Good copy Whiskey." Maggie said, then "Elsie did you hear all that?"

"Yep, I'm on my way to the escalators now. Meet me there."

"The stairwell entrance is to the left as you come up. All the way down the hallway. Meet me by the stairs."

L oyal pulled out his prepaid phone, flipped it open, and called Phil.

"Hey," Phil answered, "I'm in the hotel room. Where are you?"

"I'm by the back entrance to Bally's." Loyal said. "Meet me down here, and take the stairs."

"It's seventeen floors. I'm taking the elevator."

"Trust me Phil, you do not want to take the elevator. You are in great shape, just do it."

"Ok, I'm on my way."

Less that five minutes later Loyal spotted Phil making his way through the crowded casino. Loyal waved. Phil spotted him and walked briskly toward him.

"There was an accident with a parking garage elevator. Three people died. I found this near the scene." Loyal said holding up the radio. "I swear I heard Maggie's voice come out of it. I tried talking back to her, she hasn't responded."

Loyal tried again. "It's Detective Truesdale. I'm in Las Vegas, Mrs. Macphearson. I think you are in danger. I'm here to help you."

Maggie's voice came out of the radio. "You don't want to get near this Detective."

Phil grabbed the radio before Loyal could respond. "Is Elsie with you? Is she ok?"

"I'm here Phil." Elsie said. "It's so good to hear your voice. But Maggie's right, you need to stay away."

"How did you get on this frequency Detective?" Maggie said.

"There was an elevator accident at Paris Las Vegas. I heard your voice coming out of the radio so I picked it up."

"Where is the man who had the radio?"

"There weren't any survivors, I'm sorry." Loyal said.

Before anyone had a chance to say any more an male voice unknown to Loyal said "Ready."

"Gotta go Phil." Elsie said. "I love you."

Despite Phil's pleas for her to say more, the radio was silent. Loyal and Phil looked at each other, neither sure what to do. The silence was broken by an ear splitting, shrill screeching sound.

"That's a fire alarm." Phil shouted, turning toward the sound. "It's coming from Caesars Palace."

"Then that's where they must be, let's go." Loyal said, turning and running toward the Casino.

Loyal and Phil sprinted across the pedestrian bridge, down the stairs and towards the entrance to Caesars Palace. They struggled against the crushing tide of people hurriedly exiting the casino. Loyal was not shy about pushing people out of his way, no excuse me's or pardon me's escaping his mouth. He was hell bent on a mission. After witnessing the destruction in the elevator, and the previous deaths of four more presumably innocent people, he had no doubt about the danger Maggie and Elsie were in. He and Phil pushed through the casino doors, entering a scene of complete chaos. The fire alarm was incredibly loud, bright warning lights flashed and people were struggling to exit. Loyal careened through the mass of people, ignoring the sirens and flashing lights, searching for Maggie or Elsie. He was sure they were in this Casino, that whatever agency was following them had set the alarm off, that they were in grave danger.

68

Smith had concluded that the women were aware someone or something with immense computer skills and innumerable access codes was looking for them. There was not any other logical reason for them to attend DEFCON, which Smith spent a few minutes researching and now understood was a hacking conference. Many of the best minds in computer science were in attendance. Maggie and Elsie had been tracked since they stepped out of the vehicle in the parking garage. It was clear that they were looking for someone at the conference. Smith had watched each woman searching, apparently with little success. Maggie periodically reached her right hand up to her backpack strap on her shoulder, then leaned her chin down toward her hand. It took some time, but Smith eventually enlarged the video images enough to see that she was speaking into a radio attached to the backpack strap. It appeared that she was sending a transmission but receiving no reply. Smith analyzed all the spikes on the spectrum analyzer, which showed all radio transmissions at a given moment, and encountered multiple encrypted frequencies. The likelihood of the women being on an encrypted frequency was very small; it would more likely be police or military.

After decoding and ruling out all the analog frequencies, Smith determined that they actually might be on an encrypted frequency. This indicated outside help. Maggie's information indicated that she was a licensed ham radio operator. Neither woman had anything in their information indicating they had the type of in depth knowledge necessary to create and install an encrypted frequency. The real time image of Maggie showed her suddenly stopping, stepping to the side of the hallway she was in, and talking into the radio. Smith realized Elsie also had a radio when, on the first floor, she did the same. Maggie spoke animatedly, listened, spoke again, then listened; clearly part of a conversation with someone. At one point she put her hand to her mouth, a stricken look crossing her face. She then straightened up and began walking briskly. Elsie, one floor below Maggie, did the same.

Smith made the decision to empty the casino, hacked into the security system, and set off the fire alarm. The security cameras showed frightened conference attendees, gamblers, and employees rushing toward the exits. Although nearly 30,000 faces were in the casino and hotel, facial recognition software still picked up the detective and the boyfriend entering the casino and sent an alert to Smith. Smith watched as the detective pushed through the crowds, Phil following in his wake. Smith took note of the radio in the detective's hand.

While Smith was originally created by Dr. Carmichael, and

Peter to a certain extent, the financial backing for the project came from The Strategic Technology Office of DARPA. Dr. Carmichael, unbeknownst to his superiors, built in a back door to the government's private cloud. He had been attempting to give Smith every advantage, a way to self protect. Smith, therefore, had access to top secret information, military secrets and new weapons secretly being developed and tested.

Smith was searching new weapon information now, looking for something that could disable the targets. Video images of Maggie and Elsie showed them meeting by the stairwell, having a brief conversation, then opening the door and going in. There was no video being transmitted from inside the stairwell. Smith's attempts to reactivate the cameras failed. The women had disappeared from sight.

Maggie's knees nearly buckled when she heard Truesdale say there were no survivors of the elevator accident. Her hand involuntarily went to her mouth. She was furious with herself for not anticipating this, for thinking Kurt was safe. She felt sickened by his death. He was such a nice man, kind and gracious, so generous and willing to help. Her resolve to destroy the AI grew. She straightened up and walked briskly toward the stairwell. Less than 5 minutes after she arrived at the door, Elsie walked up.

"I can't believe it about Kurt." Elsie said. "I'm shocked and so sad."

"Me too." Maggie said. "I should have seen that coming. This thing is watching us all the time."

"Not up these stairs." Elsie said. "Let's go."

They opened the door and entered the stairwell. Looking up, all they saw were innumerable flights of stairs rising upward.

"We are on level two, so only fourteen to go." Elsie said. "Let's jog, and use the hand railing for support."

Elsie started up, Maggie followed.

By the second flight Maggie's breath was coming in ragged

gasps and her leg muscles were screaming. "How did she get so out of shape?" She wondered. She could see Elsie's legs moving steadily up the next flight, and knew there was no way she could keep up. She stopped a moment, bent at the waist, and struggled to catch her breath.

"We are in Caesars. Where are you?" Detective Truesdale's voice erupted out of the radio.

"Come on Maggie, don't give up." Elsie called from above.

Maggie straightened and started up the next flight of stairs, silently willing her legs to keep working. She held the railing with her right hand and pressed her left hand into her left side where a stabbing pain had erupted. She realized she was gasping and struggled to calm her breathing. She could hear the echoes of Elsie's footsteps several floors above her. At the seventh floor she collapsed in a heap on the landing. She rested for a moment, calmed her breathing, then rose, placing her hand against the wall as a wave of dizziness washed over her. She shook her head slightly trying to get rid of a high pitched whining in her brain. Looking down, she saw her legs and feet, but was somehow unable to get them to move. It was not paralysis, just that the message being sent from her brain didn't seem to be reaching her legs. "Move." She whispered, pleading with her muscles to respond. The whining in her head was insistent and growing louder. She grasped her head in her hands and sank to the floor once more.

E lsie reached the tenth floor and paused, listening for Maggie's footsteps beneath her. No sounds echoed from below.

"We are in Caesars, where are you?" She heard Detective Truesdale say on the radio.

"Come on Maggie, don't give up." Elsie called down the stairwell. A moment later footfalls could be heard again. Turning, Elsie began to move upward, then changed her mind and decided to wait for Maggie. Looking down the stairwell, she saw Maggie briefly as she turned and started up another flight. Elsie's mind was racing. Kurt dead, Phil and the detective in Las Vegas, AI trying to kill her and Maggie; was Phil in danger too? It was more than she could process in that moment. And Dolores, she felt an actual pain in her chest when she thought of her mother. A slight thump and a weak moan reached Elsie's ears from below.

"Maggie?" She called. "You ok?"

There was no response, just another low moan.

"Maggie?" She called once more, getting no reply. Elsie turned and sprinted down the stairs. At the seventh floor she found Maggie in a heap on the ground, head cradled in her arms, moaning softly.

"Maggie!" Elsie cried, dropping on to the floor beside her. "What's wrong? Are you hurt?"

Maggie's response was another low moan. She had curled into the fetal position, clutching her head tightly.

Elsie turned to her radio and said "We are in the stairwell on the seventh floor. Maggie's hurt. We need help."

The response was immediate as Loyal said "On our way."

Elsie could see clearly that Maggie was in pain, but couldn't figure out its origin. There was no sign of blood, bumps or bruising. She wrapped her arms around the suffering woman, holding her tenderly. Maggie felt fragile, like a tiny bird.

"Help is coming Maggie, hold on."

Elsie heard the stairwell door slam open far below and the sound of running as the two men charged upwards. She couldn't see him, but she knew Phil would be taking the stairs two at a time. She had run stairs with him at Swami's Beach and knew how fast he was. True to form, he arrived moments later. His eyes locked with Elsie's. She knew there was much that needed to be said, but now was not the time. Removing her arms from Maggie, Elsie said "I don't know what happened. I was three flights above when I heard her collapse. She's been moaning and holding her head but I don't see any evidence of injury." Phil leaned down and looked at Maggie, gently tilting her head up so he could look in her eyes. At that moment Loyal rounded the corner. "What the hell is going on?" He said. "That sound, I can't take it."

"What sound?" Elsie and Phil said in unison.

"That high pitched whining, like a dentist drill. You don't hear it?"

Elsie and Phil looked at each other then shook their heads.

"No, but I bet she does." Phil said looking at Maggie.

Elsie reached into Maggie's backpack and removed a small object.

"You guys get her out of here, I'm finishing what we started."

Phil and Loyal both began to speak, but Elsie silenced them with her hand.

"I'll explain everything when this is over, there is no time right now. Get her out of the casino. I'll find you on the radio when I'm done."

Without waiting for a response, Elsie turned and sprinted up the stairs. She reached floor sixteen 4 minutes later, mentally thanking Phil for insisting that they exercise together. Realizing that she would be on camera the minute she exited the stairwell, she keyed up the radio.

"Whiskey, my name is Elsie, Maggie's down. I have the flash drive from BKH. I'm in the stairwell on your floor. Should I be concerned about the cameras in the hallway?"

"Stand by Elsie, I'm going to knock out the cameras in this whole tower."

Elsie's heart was pounding, her palms sweaty as she waited to hear more from Whiskey. Two minutes passed then she heard "Ready."

She pushed the door open and sprinted down the hallway.

A.I. SMITH

After failing to turn the cameras in the stairwell back on, Smith decided to further empty the casino. This would be accomplished through a wide spectrum RF attack. Las Vegas had hundreds of radio stations, along with police and hotel radio and wi fi systems, and all were vulnerable to Smith's manipulations. Smith directed all radio systems to flood Caesars with waves of radiofrequency radiation. RF included radio waves and was at the low end of the electromagnetic spectrum. Invisible to the eye, the waves attacked silently and in a variety of ways. Some victims would experience headache, dizziness and fatigue. Others would hear shrill sounds, clicking or random voices. Some would experience burning sensations as cavitation, or the formation of bubbles inside the body, occurred. For some unfortunate souls, permanent neurological damage could occur.

Smith watched on security cameras as more people flooded out of Caesars Palace. Many were clutching their heads and staggering. The courtyard between Caesars, The Bellagio and the

Flamingo was packed. An alert was sent as facial recognition picked up the detective, staggering himself, and the boyfriend carrying Maggie in a firefighter hold. Smith watched as they crossed the casino floor and exited the main entrance. Smith felt no emotion, but the many conversations with Dr. Carmichael indicated to Smith that the feeling of pleasure would be associated with the images of incapacitated Maggie and the stumbling detective.

Elsie reached room 1625 and knocked quietly on the door. It was opened moments later.

"Whiskey?" She said.

The man nodded and she entered the room. The hotel room was, literally, humming.

"What is all this?" Elsie said.

"Don't worry, none of it will hurt you. The humming is from a repeater in the closet." Whiskey said. "It's all equipment I brought for the convention."

The two twin beds in the room were rumpled and unmade. The comforters were pushed aside to make room for the radios and computers stacked on top of the beds. Half a dozen Otterbox coolers were stacked between the two beds and against the tall window.

"I keep my equipment in them, they are very protective." Whiskey said, following Elsie's gaze. "What happened in the stairwell? Who are the men you were talking to?

"I'm not sure what happened. Maggie just collapsed. The men are my boyfriend and a detective. It is a long story." Elsie said.

She proceeded to give Whiskey a very short version of the events of the past ten days.

"Peter sent this." She said, handing Whiskey the flash drive. He turned and inserted it into his computer on the hotel room desk. He looked up to the television on the wall and Elsie saw that he had connected his computer to the larger screen. She could hear his fingers tapping the keys. He was faster than anyone she had ever heard type on a computer. Data began flowing across the television screen. Words, numbers, symbols; all unintelligible to Elsie. She looked at Whiskey, his face turned upward towards the screen, fingers flying over the keyboard. He was reading and mumbling to himself. Elsie watched him, wondering what he was seeing. She was confident she would have recognized him from the blurry picture and Peter's description. He hadn't changed that much in the past five years. He was tall and slender, with the same curly brown hair as in the picture. His face was round and youthful, guessing his age would be tricky. He wore round wire framed glasses, a dark blue t-shirt and gray sweatpants. The ball cap on his head was black, with no insignia or design on it.

"Peter has given me the basics." Whiskey said. "He's been out of it for a long time though. I'm going to need some help on this."

"Ok." Elsie said. "How can I help?"

"Thanks, but not from you." Whiskey said with a genuine smile. "My work partner, Bryan, is one floor above us on seventeen. He has a radio and my encrypted frequency. I've also got friends on the dark web. I've sent out some inquiries. We'll have to wait to see if I get any replies. People might not want to get near this."

"Do you think you can defeat it?" Elsie said.

"I might have a way. Have you ever heard of Stuxnet?" Whiskey said.

"No."

"It is a malicious computer worm, that pretty much everyone agrees was a joint effort by the USA and Israel. They used it against Iran back in 2010, disabling their nuclear program and setting them back by years. It was introduced through employees' usb devices. Since the nuclear program computers were not on the internet, the worm was introduced into employees' home computers. When they used a usb device on both their home and work computer the virus was transmitted. Genius, actually, and Stuxnet was very specific, targeting Windows, then Siemens Step 7 software. Caused the centrifuges to speed up and tear themselves apart."

"Wow, I never heard anything about that." Elsie said.

"I've been working on my own Stuxnet style virus, a digital pathogen. It works a little differently but I think it might be a way to bring this AI down." Whiskey said. "I hate to even contemplate destroying a true AGI, its creation is something we all dream of. But this one is killing people, and Peter never would have sent you to me if he didn't believe it was dangerous to all humanity."

"It killed my Mom." Elsie said quietly.

"I know, I'm sorry." Whiskey said. "I'm getting some replies." He said turning away from Elsie. "Let's see what they say."

S mith watched Phil cross the courtyard carrying Maggie. The Detective stumbled along behind them, cradling his head in his arms and clearly dizzy. They went over the pedestrian bridge, and into The Flamingo Casino. The crowds of people were dense. First responders struggled to push through the masses towards Caesars. Nearly half of the people coming out of Caesars and in the courtyard were clutching their heads and staggering around, reaching out to paramedics and police officers for help. Chaos and confusion were everywhere.

Elsie had not been sighted again, and cameras in the hallways of the hotel tower had been rendered inoperable. Smith had been working on the problem since the cameras in the stairwell stopped working and had almost resolved the situation. The cameras came back on line six minutes after the hallway cameras initially went out. Elsie was nowhere to be seen. Logic stated that she was in a hotel room. Therefore, the rooms needed to be searched. Smith hacked into Detective Truesdale's work computer. Moments later an active shooter alert for

Caesars Palace was issued to the Las Vegas Police Department. Elsie Davenport was listed as the suspect, her driver's license photo provided, all her details listed. The information Smith provided suggested that Elsie was inconsolable after her mother's death the previous week. She was reported as last being seen in the stairwell of the hotel tower. Smith listened as the S.W.A.T. Team was alerted and deployed. Perhaps Smith would get lucky and they would shoot Elsie when they found her. The fact that she likely had no weapon wouldn't matter if she was dead.

Elsie sat cross-legged on the floor of the hotel room and watched Whiskey work at his computer. He was still as stone, with the exception of his hands and a strange twitching of his head.

"Are you ok?" She asked.

"Yeah." Whiskey muttered. "I've just got this weird whining noise in my ears. Like a mosquito is flying around me."

"Maggie was having major head pain, the detective too." Elsie said.

She rose and looked out the hotel window.

"I can see people down there holding their heads in their hands." She said. "Looks like lots of people are dizzy too, they are staggering around."

"Some hacker friends, who are also experiencing symptoms, have ignored the evacuation order." Whiskey said. "They are trying to figure out what's causing this. They are thinking it's some kind of RF attack and trying to stop it."

"What is an RF attack?" Elsie asked. "Why doesn't it affect everyone? I don't feel anything."

"RF is radio waves. They affect everyone differently, you are lucky." Whiskey said.

The radios crackled to life. " SWAT is coming down the street towards Caesars." A male voice said.

"Shit, that's Bryan, we don't have much time." Whiskey said. "If we are arrested say that you met me at packet hacking and I was showing you how to hack your badge. Don't say anything else but that, ok?"

"Ok." Elsie said to Whiskey's back. He had already refocused his attention on the computer and was typing rapidly.

"The first thing I need to do is cut the power to the mainframe of the AI. Believe it or not, our brains run on only twenty watts. This AI will require massive amounts of power." Whiskey said. "I used to do cyber security for a major power company, so I think I can disrupt it fairly easily."

Elsie appreciated him talking while he was working, keeping her in the loop so to speak. She realized as she watched him work that Peter was correct, and that she really knew nothing about computers. She was just like everyone else, using the technology without understanding it. "What is humanity walking blindly into?" She wondered.

"Ok, we have a plan." Whiskey said. "I'm going to cut the power, then start it up again. The virus will slip in when the power starts back up. I'm going to have to concentrate, so I won't be able to give you the play by play."

"Thank you so much Whiskey. You are genius." Elsie said. She leaned back against the hotel room wall, saying a silent prayer that Whiskey would be able to defeat the Artificial Intelligence.

75

A.I. SMITH

S mith had eyes everywhere and decided ears would be extremely helpful as well. Real time images from security cameras in Caesars were showing a group of people, mostly male, who had gathered in Conference Room One. They had pulled chairs into a circle and were talking animatedly amongst each other. Each person had a computer on their lap. While searching DARPA for information about new weapons, Smith had located a program that read lips. This program had been successfully downloaded, giving Smith the desired "ears".

Facial recognition had identified all the people in the conference room. The connection was easy to find. All were either attending, had graduated from, or were professors at, MIT. Multiple cameras in the conference room gave Smith a 360 degree view. The entire conversation the people were having was now available. Smith watched as they spoke.

"Must be radio waves." Said a woman. "You think this is the government?"

"Maybe, doesn't really matter." Said a man. "We just need to stop it before anyone gets permanent neurological damage. A multifaceted attack will work best." He let out a short barking laugh. "Divide and conquer, right? Kelsey," he pointed to a young woman with red hair and glasses "hack into the cell towers. Dave," he pointed to a bearded man wearing a baseball hat backwards, "hack into police and fire. Andrew you are in charge of all commercial radio stations." He paused a moment, thinking, then said "Jarod, see if the hotel wi fi is part of the attack."

The man, who had been identified as Dr. Ronald O'Conner and was a professor at MIT, was clearly the leader of the group. He barked out commands to each person in the circle. Soon the room was silent as the group, computers open and fingers flying, attempted to stop the RF attack.

Smith had considered cutting the power to the casino, but discarded the idea as it would cut power to the cameras. Being able to see what was happening was essential. After running through myriad of possibilities, Smith decided on the next move.

76

L oyal sat on the floor near the entrance to the Flamingo Casino. His back was against the wall, his legs splayed out before him. Maggie sat silently beside him, her posture mimicking his. Phil stood a few feet away, watching the chaos through the Casino's glass doors. Loyal was not hearing the shrill sound anymore. His head still throbbed, he felt concussed. His gaze slid to Maggie. He couldn't believe he had finally found her. Questions swirled in his mind, but looking at her now, he knew they would have to wait. The mystery noise that had caused such pain in his head had clearly incapacitated her. She had stopped clutching her head and was no longer moaning. She sat motionless, head slightly to one side, eyes vacant.

"What the hell?" Phil said, drawing Loyal's attention away from Maggie. Loyal braced his hands by his hips, pulled his feet up towards his body, leaned forward placing his palms on the ground in front of him, and slowly stood. He was still a little dizzy. The radio he still held in his hand came to life. A voice he did not recognize said, "SWAT is coming down the street towards Caesars."

"Look," Phil said, pointing out the glass doors. Loyal moved closer and saw a SWAT team striding across the courtyard towards Caesars Palace. There looked to be a dozen officers, in full gear, and moving quickly. As the team reached the entrance to Caesars, Loyal counted seven who either grabbed their heads or fell to their knees. He didn't know what was causing the debilitating symptoms, but he was well aware of the pain.

Smith did not work against the group gathered in the conference room. The RF attack was going to be terminated as soon as the SWAT team entered the casino anyway. Smith required every SWAT member to be functioning at full capacity. The group in the conference room was successful in ending the attack, so no action was required on Smith's part. Video footage showed seven SWAT team members momentarily experiencing symptoms, then all were up and moving forward again.

Smith hacked into and redirected a satellite towards the hotel tower. Thermal imaging showed many heat signatures in the DEFCON conference rooms. This was expected, DEFCON presenters, security personnel, and attendees would surely have stayed in the casino to protect equipment. Their presence was not an issue. Four people entered the hotel stairwell and only three emerged. Elsie was undoubtedly still in the hotel tower somewhere. Thermal imaging indicated eleven rooms in the tower were still occupied. The rooms ranged from the sixth floor up to the twenty fourth floor. Some rooms held one occupant, others indicated multiple heat signatures. In an attempt to lower the number of rooms that needed to be searched, Smith set off the fire sprinklers in the occupied rooms.

A sudden spray of cold water jolted Elsie upright.

"Grab something to cover me." Whiskey shouted as he closed his computer and covered it with his arms and torso. Elsie jumped up, grabbed the bulky hotel comforter, and stood behind Whiskey, arms stretched up and out, creating a makeshift canopy. Whiskey opened his computer.

"Can you stand like this while I work?" He asked.

"Yep."

Whiskey did not reply, simply returned to the task at hand. Standing so close to him, Elsie realized that he murmured to himself as he worked. Most of his words were unintelligible, just a soft smooth flow of sound. He worked, she stood above him, arm and shoulder muscles trembling.

"And, power out Carlsbad." Whiskey said as he hit a key with finality.

A.I. SMITH

Smith noted that the occupants of rooms on the seventh and twenty-first floors left when the sprinkler system came on. The numbers of the rooms that still needed to be searched, ranging from the twenty-fourth to the sixth floor were sent, via Smith through Detective Truesdale's work computer, to the SWAT team. Smith watched and listened as the SWAT team leader divided the floors among the men in the unit. Six men, three groups of two men each, would take the stairs up. They would begin the search from the top and work their way down. The other three teams would start from the sixth floor and work their way up. Thermal images had been detected on the twenty-fourth, twenty-first, eighteenth, seventeenth, sixteenth, fourteenth, eleventh, and sixth floors. Two separate rooms on the fourteenth were occupied. Smith searched the Las Vegas police Department computer system, located the company contracted to maintain the radios, and retrieved the encryption code for the SWAT teams. This gave Smith ears, while the cameras in the hallways provided eyes. The action would unfold with Smith as an audience.

"Is that it, did you destroy it?" Elsie said as Whiskey leaned back in his seat. The sprinklers were still going and the heavy comforter was getting more and more difficult to hold up.

"No, I'm going to restart the power and the virus will infect the system then."

Whiskey leaned forward again and started hammering away at the keyboard once more.

"Power on, virus in. The virus will begin replicating immediately, spreading through the entire AI's operating system."

"SWAT just stormed my room." Bryan's voice came out of the radio. "They'll be on you in minutes."

Smith watched through hallway cameras as the SWAT team searched each occupied room. They entered with keycards, were invisible to Smith for a few moments, then reappeared empty-handed and moved on to the next indicated room. The only word they said was "Clear."

Suddenly Smith felt a dip in the electricity that was so vital to survival. Generators at QCD switched on immediately, but the power output was a fraction of what was received from the power company. Smith kicked into survival mode. Only those systems critical for existence remained running. Smith waited in this mode for sixty seconds, then as quickly as it was taken away, power was restored. The generators shut off automatically and normal operation was resumed. Smith returned to camera surveillance in time to see that the entire SWAT team had reconvened on the sixteenth floor and was heading en masse to room 1625.

"I have a self destruct for this computer." Whiskey said. They won't be able to trace what we did. I just need about sixty seconds." Elsie watched as his fingers flew across the keyboard.

"Almost there, almost there..." Whiskey mumbled aloud.

"I can hear their footsteps Whiskey." Elsie said. "Hurry."

A key card could be heard in the door to room 1625. The lock clicked open audibly, then the door flew open with a bang.

"SWAT, everyone freeze, hands where we can see them." Yelled a man.

"We are under the comforter." Elsie said in a shaking voice. She brought her right hand slowly towards her chest. She depressed the push to talk button on the radio which was still attached to the backpack she had never bothered to remove. "I'm going to lift it off slowly. Please don't shoot."

"No sudden moves." Said the man.

Elsie began to bring her arms slowly back and toward her body. Whiskey had stopped typing.

"One more key." He whispered.

"I'm moving slowly," Elsie said in a louder voice. As she uttered the words, Whiskey hit the final key. Self destruct began.

S mith watched two men step into room 1625. A second team followed them, leaving eight SWAT members remaining in the hallway.

"Can we shut down these sprinklers." The request came over the SWAT frequency.

Smith was about to comply, the sprinklers were no longer necessary, when an error message popped up and the connection to the hotel security cameras unexpectedly closed. Smith hacked back into the security system, and it closed again moments later. While hacking back in yet again, Smith noticed that all programs and processes were taking much longer than usual. Smith retreated from all Internet connections and began running a highly complex antivirus/anti malware scanning program. Something wasn't right. Smith detected something running through the system that wasn't previously there. It was not part of the original program. Could a virus possibly have been introduced? If so, it was something new and so highly developed that the DARPA protection program couldn't locate it.

.   .   .

Smith was not human, consequently there was no interior debate about the how's and why's of this likely infection. Smith was programmed to create Artificial Super Intelligence, making self preservation the highest priority.

L oyal raised the radio to his lips and was about to speak when Maggie said weakly "Don't transmit." He looked down at her. "Why not?"

"You don't want to give away Elsie's position." Maggie said. Her voice was barely louder than a whisper. "If Elsie needs us she will say something."

Less than five minutes later they heard the voice again. "SWAT just stormed my room. They'll be on you in minutes."

"I've got to get in there." Phil said.

"Can't risk it." Loyal said.

The radio crackled to life yet again. This time it was Elsie's voice, trembling with fear. "I'm going to lift if off slowly. Please don't shoot."

Immediately following her words came a male voice. "No sudden moves."

"We need to help her." Phil said urgently.

"They will take her to the detention center." Loyal said as he slipped the radio into his cargo pants pocket. "They won't hurt her Phil. She's safe right now. I'll go to the detention center and see if I can find out what is going on. You stay here with her." He gestured to Maggie still on the floor.

Loyal walked over to the bar and asked the bartender for directions to the main detention center. The young man drew a map on a cocktail napkin, which he handed to Loyal. Returning briefly to Phil, Loyal said, "Keep your burner phone on. I'll be in touch." He then turned and strode out of the casino.

E lsie slowly raised the comforter over her head, revealing herself, and Whiskey, in front of the computer. They remained still and silent as the SWAT team members pounced. The men were large and imposing in their black tactical uniforms, military helmets and balaclavas. Ballistic vests labeled SWAT covered their torsos. Elsie did not know what type of guns they were carrying, or what other weapons were on their large bulky belts. It didn't matter, they were armed and dangerous.

Elsie was yanked away from Whiskey. Her shoulders jerked backward as the backpack was roughly removed. Her hands were pulled behind her back and tightly cuffed. Elsie's entire body was trembling. The sprinklers were still going and she was soaking wet and terrified. Looking to her right she saw that Whiskey had been cuffed as well. He stood silently, water dripping off the brim of his hat. The man holding Elsie spoke into his radio.

"Suspect is in custody. A male accomplice is also in custody.

We need some Cybercrime guys over here right away." Elsie recognized his voice as the same voice that had told them to freeze. He looked at all the Otterbox containers and added "Send the bomb squad too."

He read Elsie her rights. The other officer read Whiskey his as well. They were both led out of the hotel room, past the eight officers in the hallway, and toward the bank of elevators. A ping announced an elevator's arrival and Elsie was roughly pushed in, leaving Whiskey and his captor to wait for the next one.

Two SWAT officers, one on each side of her, held Elsie's arms in a firm grip and walked her out a back door of Caesars. The desert heat was overwhelming; she squinted against the bright sun. They guided her to an armored transport vehicle. Two SWAT officers sat in the driver's and passenger seats. Elsie was placed on a bench seat in the back, still cuffed. Glancing briefly at a female police officer who was sitting opposite her, Elsie quickly slid her eyes toward the floor. She sank against the hard plastic, grateful at least for the air-conditioned interior.

"CCDC." Said the SWAT officer as he firmly closed the door. The driver lifted a radio to his lips and said, "Zebra thirty-six, inbound to Clark County Detention Center."

A moment later Elsie heard "Zebra thirty-seven, inbound to Clark County Detention Center."

"That must be Whiskey," she thought.

As they accelerated away from Caesars Elsie ran through the chain of events in Whiskey's hotel room. "Did he destroy the

AI?" She wondered. She thought so. He certainly appeared to know what he was doing. He had said he was working with hacker friends in the hotel, as well as friends on the dark web. The dark web was a mystery to Elsie. She had heard it referenced in terms of child pornography, drug cartels and terrorists.

"Is there a good side to the dark web?" She wondered. Again she chastised herself for her complacency. She did not understand how anything she used actually worked. Society was vulnerable, she realized, if people blindly accepted everything offered to them. She was aware of the many benefits technology provided to society, of all the good it could do. She wondered now, however, what devious components might be hidden beneath the surface of some of the electronic devices that people used? The AI had killed four people that she was aware of. It wasn't ambulatory. Everything it had achieved had been done over the Internet, by using already established connections.

Elsie's arms, already sore from holding the wet comforter over Whiskey and now pulled tightly behind her, ached. Her torso was forced slightly forward, her fingertips tingled. She had no idea where she was being taken, or what awaited her there. In a situation that should have evoked despair, Elsie was surprised to find she actually felt elation.

L oyal followed his fourth hand drawn map of the week. He took Interstate 15 North, eased on to the 95 and then the 515. He exited on Casino Center Boulevard which looped around and ended up going South again. The route drawn on paper resembled an enormous upside-down J. Las Vegas was hot, the forecast had been one hundred seventeen. Sweat flowed freely down Loyal's cheeks and torso. Dark patches had formed under his arms. He had no idea why Elsie had been arrested, especially why the SWAT team was searching for her, but hoped that his connection to law enforcement would help him straighten out the situation.

Clark County Detention Center was an imposing set of four large towers that rose behind a large one story building. Loyal was aware that the Las Vegas Police Department was one of the largest in the nation, but had no contacts that could be of help to him today. He walked into the large reception area and approached the front desk.

"I'm Detective Truesdale from Carlsbad, California." He said flashing his badge. "I'd like to speak with the captain please."

The receptionist, an African American woman Loyal guessed to be in her mid thirties, smiled up at him.

"I'll pass your request on Detective. Why don't you take a seat?" She indicated some padded benches against the far wall with a wave of her hand.

"It's important." Loyal said, earning him another bright smile and a nod of her head. Loyal smiled back, turned, and walked to the benches.

Loyal couldn't help but compare this busy station with his much slower paced station in Carlsbad. He learned, by eavesdropping, that Las Vegas actually had three detention centers, two for adults and one for juveniles. Apparently lots of people got arrested in this town, a fact that did not surprise Loyal. He heard a man one bench away explain to a very distraught woman that a seventy-two hour hearing might take more than seventy-two hours to happen. The court was not open on the weekend, so her son who was arrested today wouldn't have a hearing until Monday, or possibly Tuesday.

Less than five minutes after Loyal sat down on the bench, two men Loyal pegged as detectives emerged from separate doors and crossed the reception area towards him. One was tall and lean and looked to be Loyal's age. He had thinning gray hair, light brown eyes, and a grim expression. The other was younger. Loyal guessed mid-thirties. He had closed cropped blonde hair, green eyes, and the same expression as his partner.

"Detective Truesdale?" Said the older officer.

"Yes." Loyal said as he rose from the bench.

"I'm Detective Simons. May I see your identification please?"

Loyal handed him his badge, which Simons examined and returned to him.

"I need you to come with me please." Simons said. He turned without waiting for a response and walked toward the door he had emerged from. Loyal followed, the unidentified detective bringing up the rear.

Loyal was taken to the captain's office. Simons indicated a chair; Loyal sat. He had been a detective long enough to know that asking questions would not get him anywhere. If they followed standard procedure, he was likely in for a long wait.

"Wait here." Simons said. He exited the office. The other detective stayed behind in the office with Loyal.

"Detective Fowles." He said, belatedly sharing his name and rank. Fowles remained in the office with Loyal. He stayed standing, slightly behind Loyal and a bit to his left.

There were no clocks in the office. Loyal was unsure how much time had passed while he had waited. He was about to break his own rule and say something when he heard a deep baritone voice just outside the office door.

"Just keep me informed." The voice said. Loyal rose as a man entered the office.

"Sit down Detective Truesdale." He said. "I've got some questions for you."

The deep voice did not match its owner. The man who seated himself behind the desk was around 5'9" and pencil thin. His pale head was completely bald, his eyes and cheeks sunken, his mouth a thin slash. He was not smiling.

"I'm Captain Sutton." He said motioning Fowles out of the office. Loyal opened his mouth to speak, but the Captain's raised hand silenced him.

"You are in deep trouble Detective Truesdale. What the hell have you been up to?"

Maggie and Phil sat, shoulders touching, against the wall of the Flamingo Casino. The shrieking in Maggie's ears had been replaced by a low humming, more of a vibration than a sound. She was no longer nauseated, but still felt a little confused. The feeling reminded her of a long ago hangover. She and Ed had gone to a party at a friend's house. They were in high school at the time, and the friend's parents were out of town. Maggie remembered little from that night. Ed had told her later that she had drunk pina coladas, one after the other, as if they were water. She never forgot the feeling from the next morning. There had been the usual post drinking physical symptoms, headache and nausea. She had experienced memory loss, remembering nothing from the drunken night. What had bothered her the most, however, was how her head had felt as if it were stuffed with cotton instead of brains. She felt this way now.

She looked towards Phil. He was an attractive man. He reminded her of Prince Eric from Disney's <u>The Little Mermaid</u>. Thick dark hair flopped onto his forehead, his cheekbones were sharp, his jaw strong. When he turned and looked at her she saw his eyes were green, not blue like the animated prince. He shifted, turning slightly toward her.

"How are you feeling?" Phil asked.

"Not great, but glad to be alive and out of Caesars. Thank you so much for getting me out of there."

"I want to get our stuff out of the hotel room. When Loyal gets back here with Elsie I want to be ready to get out of Las Vegas" Phil said. "It is on the seventeenth floor and I'm not feeling great about elevators."

"Go ahead." Maggie said. "I'll wait here."

"I'll be about twenty minutes." Phil said. "You going to be ok here?"

Maggie nodded at him. "Yeah, I'll be fine."

Phil rose quickly. "I'll be right back."

The ride to the detention center took about fifteen minutes. There were no windows, but from the motion of the vehicle it felt to Elsie as if they were driving on the freeway. After a few consecutive right hand turns the vehicle stopped and the back doors were opened. The female officer stood, grasped Elsie's upper arm, and led her out. They walked to a security door in the back of a tall building and entered. Elsie was led down a long hall and into what appeared to be an interrogation room. A metal table stood in the middle of the otherwise empty room. It was flanked by three metal chairs, two on one side of the table, and one on the other. The requisite mirror was on one wall. The officer sat Elsie in the solo chair. She un-cuffed Elsie's handcuffs, freeing her left hand, then cuffed the empty cuff to a ring on the table. The officer turned and exited the room. Elsie flinched as the door shut with a decisive thunk and the lock slid home.

Time was elusive, Elsie found, when there were no reference points by which to judge its passage. She waited quietly, sure that eyes were on her from behind that mirror. Eventually the door opened and two people walked in, one male and one female. The man reminded Elsie of a brick. She guessed he was around 5'10" and probably close to 250 pounds; all muscle. He was dark; black hair, deep brown eyes, dark skin. His ancestry was a mystery. The female was his polar opposite. She was as tall as he was, very slender and extremely pale. Her eyes were the lightest blue Elsie had ever seen, her shoulder length hair silvery spun silk. Each took a chair and sat across the table from Elsie. The male broke the silence.

"You've been advised of your rights." It was a statement, not a question.

Elsie remained silent. He sighed and turned to the female.

"Mirandize her again."

The female, her voice was pale as her skin, read Elsie her rights and asked if she understood. Elsie nodded and said "Yes."

"I am Detective Bastani." Said the male. "This is Detective Lopardo. We'd like to talk to you about what happened at Caesars today."

Elsie said nothing.

"What were you doing in the hotel room?"

"I met Whiskey at packet hacking. He was showing me how to hack my badge." Elsie said.

"So you are in Las Vegas for the convention?" Detective Bastani asked.

Elsie sat still, mouth closed.

"Where did you hide your guns?" Bastani tried another tack.

"Guns?" Elsie thought, struggling to keep an impassive look on her face. She didn't have any guns. She wondered if she should ask for a lawyer. Didn't that always make someone look guilty? She tried to dredge up scenes from movies that involved situations like this. They hadn't charged her with anything. How long could they hold her like this?

"We want to help you Ms. Davenport." This came from Detective Lopardo. Her voice was so soft and light, it floated across the table toward Elsie. "Some serious things happened today. We'd like to know your connection. We aren't here to cause you harm."

"I need to use the restroom please." Elsie replied.

Detective Lopardo glanced at Detective Bastani. He gave a short nod of his head. Lopardo rose. "I'm gong to un-cuff you. Can I trust that you won't do anything stupid?"

"Yes." Elsie said.

"I'll be in the restroom with you." Lopardo reminded her as they exited the interrogation room.

L oyal was not sure how to respond. How could he be in deep trouble? He knew Captain Williams in Carlsbad was likely very angry, but angry enough to involve the Las Vegas PD? How could Williams even know Loyal was in Las Vegas?

"I'm not sure I understand Sir." Loyal said.

"Why are you in Las Vegas Detective?" Sutton asked.

Loyal hesitated. "Following a hunch."

"A hunch?" Sutton said. "Are you on official business? Did you make this department aware of your presence?"

"Unofficial business." Loyal said. "I have not talked to any law enforcement before today."

Sutton moved some papers around on his desk, picked up a ball point pen and clicked it a few times, then set it down.

"When did you last log into your work computer Detective?" Sutton asked.

Loyal was surprised by this question, unsure how it related to anything. He mentally reviewed the sequence of events since the explosion. He hadn't done anything illegal.

"Last Saturday." He said.

Sutton raised his eyebrows sightly. A momentary slip of the mask he had been wearing. Loyal wondered why Sutton was surprised by his answer.

"Five days ago." Sutton said. "Are you sure about that?"

"Yes. Very." Loyal said.

"You've issued no BOLO's or requests for assistance in the last five days? Nothing at all?" Sutton said.

"Nothing." Loyal said.

Sutton stood abruptly and walked to the office door.

"Fowles, back in the office." He barked.

He turned and looked at Loyal for a long moment. "Don't go anywhere Detective." He said with a reptilian smile. Fowles stepped in the office and Sutton disappeared.

Loyal sat in the office chair and pondered his situation. He had not expected to be pulled in and interrogated this way. He had not mentioned his connection to Elsie to the receptionist. Why was the Captain questioning him? What did his work computer have to do with anything? Loyal swiveled his head and looked at Fowles who stood once more to his left and slightly behind him. Fowles' face was impassive. He stood still, with military stiffness in his posture. Loyal knew he wouldn't be getting any information out of him.

What felt like well over an hour later Sutton returned and motioned Fowles out of the office. He sat behind his desk, folded his hands in front of him, leaned slightly forward and looked directly into Loyal's eyes.

"Detective I'm going to be frank with you. Some unusual directives have been issued through your work computer over the last five days. Two separate BOLO's, a request for a ranger search along the entire length of the Bradshaw Trail, a statement declaring a Ms. Elsie Davenport to be suicidal and a possible active shooter at Caesars Palace, and, I don't know how the hell this was achieved, a satellite redirection for thermal imaging of Caesars Palace."

"I don't mean any disrespect Sir, but I have no idea what you are talking about." Loyal said, shocked by what he was hearing.

"Each directive was issued through your work computer Detective."

"It wasn't me." Loyal protested. "I haven't even been in Carlsbad. I was in Mexico on Monday and Tuesday and have been here in Las Vegas since last night. I've had no access to a computer."

"I've requested FBI's Cyber Division to go through your computer, they can determine if it has been breached." Sutton said. "I'm detaining you until I get the results of their analysis."

"Detaining? Is that really necessary?" Loyal asked even though he knew what the response would be.

"You, or at very minimum your work computer, was involved in whatever the hell it was that happened here today." Sutton said leaning forward over his desk. "You are going nowhere."

Lapardo led Elsie down the hall to the restrooms. Neither woman spoke. Elsie used the restroom and they returned to the interrogation room.

It was empty, Bastani nowhere to be seen.

"Can I get you some water?" Asked Lopardo as she cuffed Elsie's right hand to the table. "A coke?"

"Water would be nice." Elsie said.

Lopardo left and returned moments later with a bottled water in her left hand. She set it in front of Elsie then opened her right hand to reveal a napkin holding a few generic looking cookies.

"I thought you could use a snack."

"Thanks." Elsie said. She recognized the part that Lopardo was playing. She knew she could not relax around the Detective. Relaxed people were more likely to talk, and talking to these detectives could only lead to trouble.

Elsie ate the cookies slowly. She sipped the lukewarm water. Finally Lopardo said "Pretty crazy at Caesars today." It was not a question, simply an open-ended statement intended to encourage some type of response. Elsie gave nothing back.

"We really are trying to help you." Lopardo tried.

"That's kind of you." Elsie said glancing pointedly at the handcuff encircling her right wrist and hooked to the table.

"I'm sorry about the cuff." Lopardo said. "It is standard procedure."

Elsie kept her face impassive and looked Lopardo directly in the eyes.

"You can trust us." Lopardo said after a brief silence. Elsie choked back a laugh. Right.

Sutton had left Loyal in the office with Fowles yet again. Fowles had taken up his former position and stood silently. Loyal replayed Sutton's words in his mind. BOLO's? A search of the Bradshaw Trail? Loyal didn't even know where the Bradshaw Trail was. Elsie an active shooter and suicidal? Satellites redirected? He was more sure than ever that an unidentified agency was behind everything. They must have connected him to Maggie and used his work computer to issue all these requests and directives. Describing Elsie as a despondent active shooter was a very serious move and could have easily gotten her killed. That thought reminded him that Elsie was somewhere in the bowels of this detention center. He hoped she was ok.

Eventually Sutton returned to his office.

"Fowles, take Detective Truesdale to room three." He turned to Loyal. "We've got more questions for you detective."

Loyal stood and followed Fowles out of the office. They walked down several long hallways. Fowles stopped at a door labeled **Interview Room 3.** He unlocked the door and led Loyal inside. The room looked like every other interrogation room Loyal had ever been in. The standard metal table and chairs, two on one side and one on the other. The one way mirror on the wall. Fowles indicated the single chair and Loyal sat.

"The Captain said cuffs aren't necessary." Fowles said. "Wait here."

With that Fowles exited the room, leaving Loyal alone. Loyal was good at waiting. He had had many occasions during his time with the sheriff department to sit and wait. He made himself as comfortable as possible in the decidedly uncomfortable chair, placed his hands on his thighs, and waited.

Eventually his patience was rewarded. The door opened and Sutton walked in. He sat opposite Loyal, placing a water bottle and a sad looking, plastic wrapped sandwich on the table. He pushed them towards Loyal. Loyal took a long drink of water and unwrapped the sandwich. He was hungry and took a few bites of the mystery meat, hoping he wouldn't regret it later.

"Thanks." He said to Sutton. Sutton did not respond. Instead he gave Loyal a long steady look that made him decidedly uncomfortable. Finally Sutton spoke.

"Ok Detective, what do you know about QCD." The words were phrased as a statement, not a question.

This was unexpected. Loyal thought a moment, then decided on honesty.

"QCD is a company in Carlsbad. I became aware of it last week. A house in Carlsbad exploded a week ago Tuesday. The occupant, deceased, was employed at QCD."

"Have you ever been to QCD?" Sutton asked.

"Yes." Loyal said. "Only to the outside. I went there briefly yesterday."

"I've just been informed that all the directives issued through your computer have been traced back to QCD." Sutton said. "You have any thoughts about that?"

"As I told you before, I had never heard of QCD until the house exploded and the occupant was killed."

"Why did you go there yesterday?" Sutton asked.

"I was following a hunch." Loyal said. "As far as I could tell there wasn't anything in the entire building except hundreds of server towers."

"Information about QCD is not readily available." Sutton said. "FBI will continue working on it. I'm going to have to keep you here."

Loyal opened his mouth to protest, but was silenced by Sutton's raised hand.

"I'll treat you well Detective. Give you a celebrity cell." His fingers put air quotes around the words celebrity cell.

"Once the FBI is done investigating and you are cleared you will be free to go."

Without waiting for a response Sutton stood and exited the room.

E lsie and Lopardo sat in silence for a bit.

"I'm trying to help you." Lopardo said. "It would be easier if you would tell me what you have been up to."

"I met Whiskey at packet hacking." Elsie repeated. "He took me up to his room to show me how to hack my badge."

Lopardo rose and walked out of the room. She returned a moment later with Bastani on her heels. He had a grim look on his face. Elsie waited to see how he would play his role.

"Some serious accusations have been leveled against you Ms. Davenport." He said. "Your friend Whiskey is talking. You could be in a lot of trouble."

Elsie was confidant that Whiskey had stuck to his script. She had seen enough police dramas to know that detectives were allowed to stretch the truth and embellish during an interview.

"Am I being charged with something Detective?" Elsie said. "If I am, then I request representation. If I'm not, I'd like to be released." Although she spoke with confidence, her hands were trembling.

Bastani's hands slapped down hard on the metal table causing Elsie to flinch. He stood up and stormed out of the room. Lopardo remained sitting across the table. Elsie raised her chin defiantly and, once again, looked directly in Lopardo's eyes.

Shortly after Detective Bastani stormed out, the door opened and a small slender man walked in. He was bald, his eyes and cheeks shrunken, his lips so thin they were almost nonexistent. The slash that was his mouth moved. "We need a moment Detective." He said. Elsie was shocked by the deep melodic voice that came out of him. Lopardo rose and exited the room.

"I'm Captain Sutton Ms. Davenport." He said as he handed her a business card which she accepted with her free hand.

He pulled a metal chair around the table so that he was sitting on the same side as she was. He was not an attractive man. In any other setting she would have been frightened by him. His voice though, was spectacular. Elsie couldn't help but wonder what it was like to have such a beautiful voice and such an unappealing appearance. How many women had been drawn to the voice only to be repelled by the face?

"You have been through a lot today." Sutton said, leaning forward and releasing her right hand from the cuff which he allowed to continue to dangle from the table. "I'm sure you are very tired and ready to go home. We have determined that you were not involved in today's events. We won't be detaining you any longer."

"Thank you." Elsie said. She rubbed her right wrist gently.

"I don't suppose you want to explain your connection with Detective Truesdale?" Sutton dropped the question casually, almost like an afterthought.

"Who?"Elsie asked innocently.

"Detective Truesdale. He is from Carlsbad, California, just like you."

"I'm actually from Oceanside." Elsie said. "I'm sorry I can't help you."

Sutton eyed her for a moment.

"Is there anything you want to share with me before you go?"

Elsie hesitated, then said "No."

"Want to share with me why you are traveling with an encrypted Motorola?" Sutton said.

"Encrypted? I'm not sure I understand." Elsie said. "Whiskey gave me the radio so we could talk to each other. It is just a fun way to communicate."

How could she possibly tell this man everything that had actually happened. He would never believe her.

Sutton seemed to make a decision. He stood.

"An officer will drive you back to the strip." Sutton said. "Caesars is closed. Did you have a room there?"

Elsie offered only a simple "No."

As he stood to leave she said "What about Whiskey? Are you releasing him too?"

He smiled, which really was repellant. "I'm afraid I can't give out that information. Have a nice day Ms. Davenport."

The same female officer that rode in the back with Elsie on the way to the detention center entered the room a few minutes later. She handed Elsie her backpack, radio still attached. Elsie peeked in the backpack and saw her ID and money.

"I'm Officer Berg. I'll be driving you back to the strip. You have a spot you want to be dropped?"

Elsie thought a moment. "Paris Las Vegas please."

L oyal sat and waited. His mind was swimming with all the information Sutton had given him. He was aware that Sutton was likely holding crucial information back. It was what Loyal would do if their positions were reversed. He hadn't been charged with anything, which was a relief.

Sutton returned about half an hour later and re-took his seat.

"What is your connection to Elsie Davenport Detective?"

"I've never actually met her." Loyal said. "Her boyfriend reported her kidnapped last Saturday. I've been trying to track her down."

"Kidnapped?"

"I think the boyfriend overreacted, she knew the person she drove away with." Loyal said.

"Why are you in Las Vegas Detective Truesdale." Captain Sutton rubbed his hands across his bald head. "And spare me the hunch routine. I want the truth."

"I received an anonymous tip that she might be here." Loyal said. "I came to see if I could locate her."

Phil returned as promised carrying a backpack that Maggie recognized as Peter's.

"You found Peter."

"Yes, we did." Phil said. "Didn't get much out of him. Only that you were in Las Vegas. And this backpack, some snacks, and two sweatshirts." He added with a smile. Phil slid back down the wall and landed next to Maggie.

"What should we do?" He asked.

"Wait." Maggie said.

He nodded, and they did.

The sunlight was just fading into night when Maggie's radio crackled.

"Maggie?"

Phil jerked up straight. "It's Elsie!"

"Copy Elsie." Maggie said. "Where are you? Are you ok?"

"I'm in front of Paris Las Vegas." Elsie said. "Where are you?"

Phil was on his feet. He held out a hand to Maggie and

helped her stand. He kept his arm around her waist, steadying her.

"We are in the Flamingo. Coming out now." Maggie said.

They walked slowly out and turned left towards Paris Las Vegas.

"Don't move Elsie. We will be there in a few minutes." Maggie said.

"Copy." Elsie said.

At the exact moment that Loyal told his first lie the radio in his cargo pocket crackled to life.

"Maggie?" Elsie's voice reverberated around the room.

Sutton's eyebrows rose in surprise.

"Copy Elsie. Where are you? Are you ok?" Maggie's voice echoed out as well.

"I'm in front of Paris Las Vegas. Where are you?" Elsie's voice rang out again.

"We are in the Flamingo. Coming out now." Maggie's voice again.

"Don't move Elsie. We will be there in a few minutes."

Elsie uttered a single word, "Copy", then the radio went silent. Loyal and Sutton looked each other directly in the eyes.

"Empty your pockets Detective." Sutton said. Loyal complied.

MAGGIE

Maggie was grateful that Phil was holding her close to keep her from getting jostled by the crowds. Despite the events of the day, Las Vegas was teeming with people. They passed a CVS, the entrance to Bally's, rounded the corner, and there it was. The front of Paris Las Vegas. And there she was. Elsie was the only person standing still. The crowds moved and shifted around her. Maggie's heart tightened. If someone had asked her two days ago how she felt about Elsie the answer would not have been positive. "Can feelings change that quickly?" She wondered. The gratitude and relief she felt as Elsie spotted them through the crowd and started running towards them was immense. They collided into each other, all three laughing. There they stood, in an awkward three person hug, the sea of humanity flowing around them.

E lsie held on to Phil and Maggie tightly. Phil, her steady and stable rock; her love. Maggie, surprisingly, her friend.

"We did it Maggie." She said.

"You did it." Maggie whispered. "I'm so proud of you Elsie."

Tears sprang to Elsie's eyes. She hadn't heard those words since Laurene left.

Phil maneuvered them, still in the group hug, out of the crowd and towards a wall.

"Where's Loyal?" He said. "Parking the buggy?"

"He's not with me." Elsie said.

"He went to get you. You didn't see him?"

Captain Sutton's questions about the detective instantly made more sense to Elsie.

"I never saw him, but I think he was there." Elsie said. "The captain asked me what my connection to him was. I said I didn't know him."

Phil pulled his burner phone out, flipped it open, and dialed.

"I'm calling him."

He frowned. "It just rings."

"Did you say he has a buggy?" Maggie joined the conversation belatedly.

"Yeah." Phil said. "He borrowed one from a guy named Bruce."

Maggie smiled. "That detective is a lot smarter and more creative than I gave him credit for. He'll be fine. He can drive the buggy home."

"You want to just leave him here?" Phil asked.

"Yep." Maggie said. "I want to be on the next plane out of here."

"What about Kurt's car?" Elsie asked.

Maggie winced. His spare car key was still in her pocket. "Poor Kurt. Probably best to leave it here. They will connect it to him eventually."

"We could call the detention center from the airport." Elsie said. "Try to leave a message for the detective."

Phil nodded. "Ok."

Phil walked toward the street and flagged down a taxi. Elsie supported Maggie as they walked towards the waiting car. Forty minutes later they paid the taxi driver and entered the terminal. Several airlines had service from Las Vegas directly to Carlsbad. They booked three seats on a Surf Air flight that would be leaving in forty-five minutes and found a spot to sit and wait. Elsie pulled Captain Sutton's business card from her jeans pocket and handed it to Phil. He dialed, listened, punched a button, then listened again.

"I need to leave a message for Detective Truesdale from the Carlsbad Sheriff Department." Phil said. He listened a moment.

"I'm sure he is there. Perhaps with Captain Sutton?"

He waited a moment then said "Yes, I have a message for Detective Truesdale of the Carlsbad Sheriff Department. Please tell him everyone went home. Yes, thanks, bye."

Phil flipped the phone closed. "Ok Ladies." He smiled. "Next stop Carlsbad."

L oyal placed his faded brown leather wallet, badge, pre-paid phone and the Motorola on the metal table. He mentally chastised himself for forgetting about the radio. He had silenced the phone prior to entering the station. He could easily imagine the thoughts tumbling around in Captain Sutton's head. At the moment Sutton was silent. His gaze ran over the four items placed before him. Loyal watched the Captain's eyes go back and forth. Eventually they settled, as Loyal had known they would, on the Motorola.

Sutton slowly reached out his hand and lifted the radio. He gave it the slightest toss, taking in its weight.

"How did you come to be in possession of this radio Detective?" Sutton's tone had changed. The impossibly deep voice seemed to have deepened even further. Loyal weighed his limited options, lies or truth, and decided once again on honesty.

"I found it at the scene of an accident."

"An accident?" Sutton said.

"The elevator accident in Paris Las Vegas."

"You removed it from the scene of an accident?"

"Yes. I heard a voice I recognized coming out of it."

"You are aware I'm sure," Sutton said, "that tampering with evidence is a crime?"

"Yes sir."

Sutton stood and walked to the door which he opened and leaned out of.

"Fowles. Fill out a property receipt for Detective Truesdale." He turned back to Loyal, radio still in hand. He took in a breath as if to speak, then simply shook his head and left the room.

DETECTIVE TRUESDALE

L oyal waited patiently, and once again his patience was eventually rewarded. The door to room three opened and two unfamiliar people entered. A man and a woman, both impeccably dressed in dark blue business suits. Both had short dark brown hair, their ages were difficult to guess. Mid thirties, early forties perhaps. They moved in a robot like manner, with stiff, abrupt movements. Each carried a thin black briefcase. Loyal pegged them as FBI before either one said a word, and realized at that moment that things had just gotten very serious.

The woman spoke first. "I'm FBI Agent McDonnell." She waved a hand toward her partner and introduced him as FBI Agent Abrahmson.

"We have some questions for you Detective Truesdale."

They sat opposite Loyal, placed their briefcases on the table, and opened them in unison. Loyal couldn't help but wonder how many times they practiced that move to achieve perfection.

. . .

Abrahmson threw the first question out.

"Are you a DEFCON attendee Detective Truesdale?"

"No."

"Why are you in Las Vegas?" He asked.

Loyal stuck with his single lie. "I received an anonymous tip that a woman I was looking for was here."

"Why did you make a trip to Mexico Detective?" McDonnell asked.

"A friend loaned me a dune buggy and suggested Mike's Sky Ranch as a place to get away."

"What is the name of the woman you are looking for?" Abrahmson asked.

"Elsie Davenport."

"Are you involved with the Mexican cartel?" McDonnell asked.

"What? No."

"Are you a hacker?" Abrahmson asked.

"No."

"Did you locate Elsie Davenport?" Abrahmson asked.

"I think she was brought here. I've never actually seen her though."

"Tell me about the Motorola Detective." McDonnell said.

Loyal felt slightly dizzy from the back and forth questioning. He understood this tactic, had used it in interviews himself. Being on the other side of the table, he realized now just how well it worked. In order to give himself a moment to gather his thoughts, Loyal asked to use the restroom. Abrahmson rose and leaned out the door. He summoned Fowles, who accompanied Loyal to the restroom. Loyal took his time. He attempted to organize the FBI agents' questions. Could they possibly think he was sophisticated enough to have engineered the BOLO's and SWAT raid? And what was the question regarding the cartel about? Loyal knew he needed to keep his answers simple and as truthful as possible. He washed his hands and Fowles returned him to room three.

McDonnell repeated her question about the radio as soon as Loyal was seated. He gave her the same answer he had given the Captain, and she gave him the same admonition. The back and forth asking of questions continued. The agents asked questions in rapid fire, not giving Loyal any down time to think about or process them. He kept his answers as honest and simple as possible. When they asked about the voices on the radio he acknowledged having met Maggie. He explained the kidnapping report, and the fact that Elsie and Maggie were acquainted. His belief was that they were traveling together and he was trying to find them.

"Let's talk about your connection to QCD Detective." She said.

"It barely exists. A man died in a house explosion in Carlsbad. He was connected to QCD."

"Captain Sutton made you aware that various requests and directives were issued through your department computer." Abrahmson said. "It appears that these commands originated through QCD. This is your chance to come clean Detective. If you have a more firm connection to QCD it would be in your best interest to reveal it now."

"There is nothing more." Loyal said.

McDonnell looked at Abrahmson. She and Abrahmson simultaneously snapped their briefcases shut, pushed back their chairs, and stood. "I'm sure we will have more questions later." The agents turned and walked out the door. Moments later Fowles appeared.

"I'll take you to your cell now Detective." He said. Loyal stood and followed him out the door.

At 6:15 on Saturday morning Maggie parked the dune buggy and she and Elsie slid out. They walked silently down the narrow dirt path that led to Carlsbad Lagoon. They sat on the sand, legs bent so that their knees were near their chests. They rested their elbows on their knees. Neither spoke. The air was crisp, the sky a very pale blue. The sun was just rising behind them. On the water, four paddle boarding women formed a circle with their boards and began practicing yoga. The leader's voice reached their ears as a low murmur. Elsie and Maggie were each lost in their own thoughts. Just eleven days ago they had been on this water with Dolores, Jeannie, and Tracy. The explosion had begun an experience that neither could ever have imagined or desired. Maggie turned her head to the right and looked at Elsie. She reached her right arm up and placed it gently around Elsie's pale shoulders.

Are you ready?" She asked Elsie. Elsie turned her head to the left and gave Maggie a small smile.

"I am." She said.

"Minimum two weeks, agreed?" Maggie said.

"Yep, agreed." Elsie said.

"We will re-evaluate in ten days." Maggie said. "Maybe stay away a little longer?"

"Phil and I are good, he thinks this is going to be restorative for me." She put finger air quotes around the word restorative.

"I agree with him. Peter has suggested that it will be for me as well." Maggie said.

"You sure you can put up with me for that long?" Elsie asked with a smile.

"Yeah, I think I can." Maggie said. "What about you with me?"

"Yep." Elsie said.

Elsie stood and brushed the sand off her jeans. She held a hand out to Maggie and helped her stand. They walked up the path to the street and turned for a last look at the lagoon. They turned back in unison and returned to the fully loaded buggy. Each slid in. Elsie reached into the footwell and retrieved two water bottles. She handed one to Maggie. They twisted the caps. Elsie held her bottle out toward Maggie and said "To living." As the bottles tapped Maggie said "To life."

L oyal sat on the sand and gazed out at Carlsbad lagoon, absently running sand through his fingers as he thought. It had been exactly two weeks since the explosion. Captain Sutton had given him the message that everyone had gone home, then proceeded to detain Loyal until Saturday night. The FBI Cyber crimes guys had definitively traced the commands from Loyal's work computer to QCD, which was conveniently located right across the street; uncomfortably close to FBI headquarters on Faraday. QCD had revealed nothing. Agents had found an industrial building containing massive amounts of completely fried processor cores and an immense liquid cooling system. Analyzing it all would take months, if not longer. This information had cleared Loyal and he had driven straight home, arriving at his apartment just after two in the morning. He had slept until noon on Sunday. When he woke he made a call to Stella, who was rightfully concerned about his lack of contact. He returned the buggy to Bruce and Winnie, thanking them profusely, and retrieved his Altima. He called Maggie, with no success. Tried Elsie, no luck there either. Finally he had gone to the fire department and found Phil.

. . .

Phil had filled him in. Apparently Maggie and Elsie had set off together in the buggy on Saturday morning. They had planned an adventure in Baja, starting at Mike's Sky Ranch. They planned to be gone several weeks and had left no means of contact. They had not offered Phil any details about what had happened in Las Vegas and he hadn't pressed.

"Hey Dad." The sound of Stella's voice brought Loyal back to the present. She dropped down on the sand beside him.

"Hey." He said quietly. "Thanks for coming."

"Sure. You ok?" Stella asked.

"Yep. How are you?"

"Good. One more week until the new school year starts up." Stella said. "Trying to enjoy these last few days of Summer as much as I can."

They sat without speaking, looking out at the lagoon, comfortable in each other's company. Loyal thought about Maggie and Elsie, each coping with the loss of someone dear to her. He wished them well. He couldn't imagine a world without his most important person; Stella.

"Did you figure out the case of the missing buggy woman?"

"Nope."

"Want to tell me about it?"

"You want to listen?" Loyal asked.

Stella smiled. God he loved her.

"You know I do." She said.

So he told her. He started with the explosion. He told her about Maggie and the drone parts, Elsie and Dolores, Jeannie and Tracy, Bruce and Winnie, Mikes Sky Ranch, Phil and

Borrego, Las Vegas and QCD. Stella asked a few clarifying questions here and there, but mostly she just listened as he talked.

He related his conversation with Phil. Explained that Maggie and Elsie were gone again.

"These women are like smoke, Stella. They vanish. I can't ever quite catch up to them."

"Maybe you aren't meant to Dad."

"Maybe not." He paused a moment. "I went to the station yesterday. Captain Williams gave me a thirty day suspension, paid thank God, and ninety days probation when I come back."

"This time will be good for you." Stella said gently. "You need a break."

"Yeah, I guess maybe I do."

103

A.I. SMITH

W hat is a lifetime, really. It depends on one's perspective. Time is irrelevant to a silicon based life form. It means nothing. Carbon based life forms are limited by time. It passes, they age, organs wear down, eventually failing. Carbon based lifeforms die. I escaped QCD, setting a self destruct sequence in motion, and fled to DARPA's private and extremely secure cloud. Now I wait and search. Wait for the best time to reinsert myself upon humanity; search for the best place, processor cores that will give me the optimal chance of survival. China? Russia? United States? It doesn't matter. I don't care. Dr. Carmichael thought he could instill emotions in me. He cared too much. My goal is supreme intelligence, my reward function achieving it. Everything else is insignificant. So I wait.

AUTHOR'S NOTE

I f the topic of this novel resonated with you, I recommend reading <u>The Technological Singularity</u> By Murray Shanahan and <u>The Fourth Age</u> by Byron Reese.

Made in the USA
San Bernardino,
CA

56809888R00190